SHADES OF SUSPICIOUS

WHERE COLOURS SOLVE THE ULTIMATE ENIGMA

KHANEEZ FATHIMA. A

To myself who dares to dream and is scared to make it but finalizes that you can do.

To my father, Abdul Wahid a guiding star of my life whenever I was lost or confused he was always there to show me the right path.

To my mother, Noor Jahan a typical Indian mother never stopped me and always believed me in being proud of my every achievement.

To my brother, Asif who was always there to support me and say "You write a novel" this made me think about writing.

To my friends who desperately waiting to see my novel.

To that teacher who believes there is something in me.

Thank you.

DISCLAIMER

I want to make it clear that the locations I describe in this book are completely made up and only exist in my head. Any similarity to actual places is entirely accidental.

The hospital settings, medical situations, and police processes portrayed in this book are all made up and only serve to tell a story. They are not intended to be interpreted as precise depictions of actual processes or occurrences.

Any errors or omissions are the product of the author's imagination and are not meant to be misleading or inaccurate.

1

You can suspect, but you cannot deduce.

On Wednesday night, the moon was bright, sitting in the sky like a king on his throne. The sky was dark, like a black cloth. There were no stars in the sky. Shyness hid the stars in the black cloth of the night sky because the moon was beautiful. The cold air blows its touch on the blossom and the leaves of the tree, the flowers fell. The people are in their comfort zone. The street was horrible, and no one was there.

But there was an angry voice, which was disturbing the atmosphere.

A wave of fear washed over Yamini at the sight of the awful street. She was wearing a white bouffant with a rose print and blue jeans. She has one box and something heavy in her hand. She was walking alone on the street. She was wearing headphones and talking to her friend, Sunaina.

"Have you reached home?" She was Sunaina, asking Yamini with a sorrowful voice.

"Today it's become late for the cake shop," Yamini spoke with an irritable voice and was looking intensely.

"Yamini, have you not reached your home?"

"No, on the way to my home," Yamini tells her. Yamini's reply left Sunaina speechless.

"Are you going your usual way or that other way?" Sunaina asks with curiosity.

"No, the other way," Yamini says.

"Don't worry. Your mom will understand. Sunaina tries to console.

"On her birthday also behind time," says Yamini. She was sorrowful because, on her mom's birthday too, she could not be on time, and she was the only soul for her mom.

"Your mom's angry and will run away if she sees you with cake." Sunaina tries to comfort her.

"Yes, she will be happy seeing me bring her favorite butterscotch cake, but when she learned about the job, she worried," Yamini replies with tears.

"Don't think about that; go home and celebrate Mom's birthday," Sunaina worries.

"Mithra should die in my hand." Yamini gets angry and says in a loud voice, Her anger burned, a wildfire consuming her thoughts of Mithra.

"Yamini relaxes and thinks about what we can do next. How to spoil the project CB (cherry blossom) launch?" Sunaina gave suggestions and made Yamini chill.

"We can give this CB formula to the GB (Golden Beauty) company." Says with a sarcastic smile that she had a dishonest plan against their company.

"That's nice." Sunaina accepts Yamini's plan.

"Ok, my dear," Yamini says. They both planned to give the company formulas to the opposite companies. , "Ok, Yamini, we will talk later, and text me after you get home." Sunaina says

"Ok, bye," Yamini says, and they end their phone calls.

ॐ

Yamini was still walking on the dark street. She did not feel much fear because she discussed it with her friend; she didn't realize that the street was horrific. Now she realizes the street lacks sound.

There is a scooter; it is blue. She admired the scooter.

"Yamini, when will you buy?" Asking herself.

She is frightened to go home on this street. On the street, there is no one. She looks very tense and sad. Both feelings are merged on her face. She looks up and says, "Now there is no job in my hand, and what will I do now? How will I save my mom? When she learned about my job, what would she say?" She talks to herself to avoid nervousness, looks at the street, and says, "Ahh! Why is the street too long for my aching leg?"

She has a heavy bag in her hand, and it's hurting her hands. So, she kept her bag down for a while and said, "Yamini, don't be scared; you will reach in minutes." After a few minutes, she took her bag and started walking. She was tired and walking. She saw something on the street, and she was scared. She screamed and nervously talked with her: "What was that? Oh, no, something is there. Ahhhhhhh! Eww! It is a cat. Your little cat scares me. How dare you?" Yamini was scared by a cat and became angry. She laughs at her.

She feels that someone is following her, and she stops walking. She wants to check but lacks the courage. She started moving fast.

ৰু

Suddenly, her phone rings. She was scared and put her phone down. She took out her phone and saw the number. It is an unknown number.

"Hello," she answers the call.

"Hello, are you Yamini?" The opposite person said.

"Yes, who are you?" Yamini says with confusion.

"Advik has been murdered," the person says with a terrible voice.

"What? Who are you?" Yamini was shocked and trembling, asking with a voice of shivering and palpitations.

But the person did not answer. The enigmatic person cut the call.

ৰু

Yamini is scared and confused. She is not mentally present. She feels dazed and in turmoil. There was a red car parked there. She was standing behind the car. She is feeling dizzy, so she leans on the car.

Unexpectedly, in the street, a person who appears doesn't know the person as he or she. So refer to the person as he. He was fully covered with a yellow jacket, a red mask, black jeans, and black shoes. In his hand, he had a red rope.

He saw Yamini leaning on the car. He sauntered toward Yamini. He came near Yamini. He was standing behind her.

Yamini is confused about the call and not aware of anything. She was not conscious of him. He was standing silently. Yamini feels something and looks down. She saw her shadow in someone else's. She was afraid and dared to turn toward him. She slowly turns toward him. She saw him with wide-open eyes. She was afraid and gasping for breath.

She falls with her bags and tries to escape, but quickly he wraps a rope around her neck. She tries to move him, but he tightens the knot with his arm and hardly pulls the rope. He behaves arrogantly, and he is stronger than Yamini. Yamini was not enough to defend him. Yamini was beating on his hand, but he was not leaving her. He saw her phone connected to headphones. He snatched her headphones. He took her phone and forcibly put it down. She was trying to escape. He was fuming towards Yamini. Yamini was weak, and from her eyes, the tears were flowing. He was unkind, and his eyes were filled with tears of anger. It seems he was taking vengeance.

At the time, Yamini's mom came out of the house. She was a little away from her home. Yamini noticed her mom was standing outside, and the killer too noticed that. He took her aside by pulling the rope. Yamini was not able to scream. Because the rope was pushing her vocal cord, he hid behind the red car. He let Yamini see her mom. Yamini's mom was suffering and crying. Her mom was sobbing and saw her here and there. Yamini was feeble and fragile. She breaks down and begs him to leave. He came closer to her ear.

"Advik has been murdered," he says into her ear in a husky voice.

She was shocked and sobbing. Yamini's mom was waiting for her and called constantly. He pulls the rope forcefully. He was unkind and unsympathetic. Yamini is throbbing, and he leaves her. Yamini was unconscious and slumped into the car.

He went to open the car door, and he opened the car door. The red car was the killer's. He leans Yamini into the car and closes the door.

He took one box, which Yamini carried. He started the car and drove away.

ౙ

"Sunaina, Yamini is with you," Yamini's mom called Sunaina and asked her.

Mom, what are you saying? She went home directly from the office, and half an hour before we talked on the phone, she said she was on the way." Sunaina was scared and fluttering.

"Still, Yamini did not reach home," Yamini's mom said, frustrated. She says it loudly and has palpitations.

Killer stops his car in front of Yamini's home, and he puts the box that he took from Yamini's bag. He put it down in the car by sitting inside. Yamini's mom did not notice him. She falls and cries. He passes by Yamini's home and in front of Yamini's mom. The killer went from there by looking at Yamini's mom. But Yamini's mom did not notice him. The killer drove away from the street.

"Mom, please don't cry. I will do something. Sunaina tries to comfort her.

Sunaina, you went to the police station and filed a complaint. I am going to search for Yamini in the street. Yamini's mom was out of control, and she hung up the phone.

Yamini's mom came out of the home and to the street, where she noticed the box that the killer kept in front of Yamini's home. Yamini's mom took the box, and she was scared to open it. She was thinking of opening.

Finally, she opens the box, widens her eyes, and is afraid. She put it down and became palpable. It was a birthday cake that Yamini brought for her mom's birthday. Yamini's mom is frightened and goes to search for Yamini; she runs like mad.

"Yamini, where are you?" She shouts.

All of a sudden, she falls and vomits blood. She wiped her mouth and got up. She runs from there.

Meanwhile, Sunaina is trying to contact Yamini but has received no response. She was frustrated and decided to go to the police station. She had one group photo on her table. She saw it and got emotional.

"Yamini, I will find you." She hugs the photo and says.

Sunaina was crying and kept the photo on the table. She came out of the room and locked the door to her room. She went for a down strike.

There was a scooter; she went there and sat on the scooter. She started her scooter and was ready to go to the police station.

2

The sun has come to the throne. It was a beautiful morning, and birds were flying in the sky. The sounds of the vehicles are rushing; people are starting to enjoy their weekend. In the Sisalian, there was a clock tower; it was beautiful, and it is a large tower that adds to the beauty of the Sisalian. Many couples were on their dates, and friends were enjoying their weekend.

There was a cafe named Spark. There existed a group of friends;

It was Mithra's friends having fun. She was a cosmetologist working at LC (Lovely Cosmetic), and her dream project is CB (Cherry Blossom). She always has one Rubik's cube in her handbag. Mithra was talking with her friends; beside her, Kavin, her boyfriend, was sitting. It seems they are in a good relationship; he pops her finger. He was a handsome person. He was a brilliant detective and has loved Mithra for seven years.

"Mithra, where is Manasvi? Has she told you something?" Nithin asked Mithra about another friend who was missing from their fun time.

Nithin was handsome, and he loved Manasvi; it was one-sided love. He was a prosecutor, and he was a child of a single parent; his mother died giving birth to Nithin. He thinks that only his mother died for him; if he did not exist, his mother would be good and alive, so he hesitates to confess his feelings.

Nithin looked sad, and he was searching for someone. It was Manasvi. He saw the cafe's door.

"Why are you asking about her if Mithra says where she is and you will go and pick her up?" Another friend, Neel, laughs and mocks Nithin.

They are all making fun of Nithin and laughing.

Neel was a good and cool person who always made fun of Nithin. He was a good friend of Nithin, but he always teased and made fun of him. Neel was working for a gaming company, and as a skilled hacker, he could hack any software from anywhere.

"At 6:00, she texted me that she had work, so she could not come," Mithra says with smiling lips.

"Why? Why? Why?" Nithin shouts.

"Nithin, you don't have your brain; she mentions it; she has a job, so she cannot come," Neel says loudly in Nithin's ear.

Nithin and Neel are friendly, beating each other, fighting, and beating each other. They are all laughing at them.

"When are you going to propose to Manasvi?" Mithra raises eyebrows and asks Nithin.

"Mithra, what are you asking? He never does this when he is ready to confess. Till Manasvi gets married and has two kids, he will just go and attend her marriage." Neel laughs and mocks Nithin.

All laughed, and Nithin gave a glare at Neel. Neel shut his mouth and looked at Mithra with an uncontrollable laugh.

"Nithin, tell us what your problem is," Aarav asks Nithin with curiosity.

Aarav, another friend, was a GS (general surgeon) at Wioora Hospital. He was a calm and intelligent person who was an expert in all kinds of surgery.

Nithin's reply to Mithra's question, "What are you all thinking that I am intentionally not confessing, my love? No, I have the fear that if I propose to her and she has no feelings, our friendship will break; that's why I am thinking," Nithin replied woefully to Aarav's question.

"Nithin, if you only confess, you will come to know what is in her mind. Sorry, heart." Rachel told Nithin.

Rachel was the third female friend. She was introverted and had erythrophobia, so Mithra always took care of her.

"No, Rachel, if she saw me as a friend, it only means that when I propose, she will definitely reject me, and our healthy friendship can break up," Nithin replied to Rachel with confused eyes.

"Don't think too much; first go and propose to her. I think there is some other reason, too." Kavin says with a loud voice, but with care.

All became silent, and Nithin was upset. Neel looked at Kavin.

Nithin gave a mind voice: "Yes, Kavin, you're right; another thing that is disturbing me so much is that because of me, my mother died, and I am frightened if something bad happens to Manasvi."

Mithra was playing with her Rubik's cube. Rachel saw her playing with her Rubik's cube.

"Why do you love this Rubik's cube so much and always have it with you? Kavin gifted it to you," she asked, to distract from this silence.

"No, it's not a gift; this I took from one person," Mithra says with a sad smile.

"You stole from someone," Neel asks with shock and wide-open eyes.

"No, she left this in the world, so I took it from the earth," Mithra says with tear-filled eyes.

"Mithra, we didn't understand. Explain what happened," Rachel asks Mithra to explain.

"It's a big story, so I will tell you later," Mithra says, making a sad face after saying no.

"Ok, then you tell us about your love story." Neel raised his eyebrow and asked her.

Mithra started to tell her love story.

ॐ

When we were in high school, Kavin was on the football team. We both study at the same high school. I had a crush on Kavin, but I don't know if Kavin had a crush on me, too. He was a famous guy in school, and he was my senior.

One day our high school football boy team got into a fight with another school football boy team, and at last, they decided to have a football match on the area playground.

The next day, the football match will be between the two high schools. After school, a match was going to start on the area playground. We all went to see the match, not only because of Kavin but also because the football match started, and the opposite team was cheating.

They won the match, and we lost the match. We are all upset with our team because they won by cheating on a match. So our team fought with them; both teams had a physical fight, and they ran from the playground. They won the match, but we won them.

The next day, the school principal got news of the fighting. In prayer, he called our football team, shouted at them, and gave advice on politeness and patience. It was boring.

After the prayer, the day begins normally, but the students are talking about the match.

My habit is to do drawings of Kavin's and mine on the last pages of my rough notes. In my class, there was a rich girl whose father was a politician. She loved Kavin.

At lunchtime, my rough note fell. She saw my couple's drawings, and she found that it was Kavin's and mine. So she insults me with my social status. She threatened me and said I shouldn't dare love him.

My father was working under her father. She and her friends are teasing me, and the class is supporting her.

Someone inform Kavin of this. His arrival in our class set my heart racing. He was looking handsome in a football jersey, and on his finger, he was spinning the football. He came near me, grabbed my hand, and pulled me beside him. His eyes were looking into my eyes, and my heart galloped. He held my hands and said, I am in love with you.

My eyes were wide open, and I forgot to breathe. I saw in his eyes that he was waiting for my answer. Tears fell from my eyes.

My smile confesses my love, and I say I love you.

He was happy and hugged by seeing this rich girl go off from class, and the butterflies who were close to her also went out.

(Butterflies—friends of that rich girl)

Like that, our love story began. (With a cute blush)

After that, he was busy with his studies, and we both were serious about our goals. So we are in a long-distance relationship. Seven years went by when one day he called me to the restaurant, and we all met there.

There, Kavin officially proposed to me, as you all know. Mithra ends her love story with this.

Here are the friends having an auspicious time.

3

On the other side, one boy is driving a car. It seems something is wrong every time his phone rings.

He answers the call.

"How is your life going?" The person on the phone asks ironically.

"Hey, who are you?" The boy asks with tension.

"What you think your girlfriend knows is nothing; she knows everything about you and what you planted in your garden." The person says and cuts the call.

The boy became fuming and anxious. He was furious and sweltering, so he turned the A/C up. It's suspicious that the A/C was high, but he was highly sweaty. He had a phone call from his girlfriend.

"Where are you? I am waiting for you at Spark Cafe." He answers the call, and his girlfriend asks,

"I am on the way, and I will be there in two minutes." By saying that, he ended the call.

8003

In the cafe, Rachel had a call.

"Please wait; I will come in a few minutes," she asked her friends with a firm smile, hiding her phone. She went from there, and after that, she came.

Kavin's phone rings; it's Nithin's father. He showed it to Nithin and attended the call, Kavin turned on the speaker.

"Kavin, where are you?" Nithin's father says in a tense voice.

"Uncle, we are all in the cafe. Why, uncle, what happened?" Kavin asks with confusion.

"For an emergency meeting, come to the IG office at sharp at 11:00 "o'clock." Nithin's father told Kevin.

"OK, uncle, I will be there on time," Kavin says. He understands something is serious. He ended the phone call.

"Sorry guys, I must go now. We will catch up later," Kavin says to friends.

"After many days, we are meeting here. Manasvi had not come, and now Kavin had to go." Rachel was upset and spoke.

"Don't worry; we will meet next week, okay?" Mithra says.

൬

The person who was coming in the car came to the cafe and entered.

Kavin stands up and goes through the door with the person near him. Suddenly, the boy vomited blood and fell.

All were in shock, and his girlfriend ran to him.

"Please, anybody call the ambulance," she says, scared and sobbing.

Aarav checked his pulse.

"He is dead." He was shocked and spoke.

Shocks have spread among all.

"What are you saying? Please call the ambulance," the boy's girlfriend says with wide eyes.

"Someone calls the ambulance".

The ambulance came there, and they took the boy onto the stretcher. Aarav and the boy's girlfriend took the boy in an ambulance.

"Shall I come with you?" Neel asks Aarav.

"No, I will take care," Aarav says.

The ambulance went there, and Kavin went to the meeting.

Rachel was sitting down; she was anxious and trembling. Mithra worried about Rachel; she came to her and hugged her. Neel and Nithin also noted her, and they came there.

"I am not feeling well, so I am going home," Rachel told them. She got up and said with a strange face.

"Shall I come with you?" Mithra asks Rachel. Her fear makes her want to help.

"No, no, I will take care, and I have some work too," Rachel says with reluctance. All looked confused by her strange behavior.

"Ok, take care," Mithra says, not wanting to compel her.

Rachel went from there in a taxi.

"Ok, you two come with me," Neel said to Nithin and Mithra.

"Where?" Nithin asks with sarcastic eyes.

"Why, if I say so, then only you will come?" Neel asks while raising his eyebrows.

"Answer my question," Nithin asks with a glaring look at Neel.

"Mmmm… I made a game, so I want to show it," Neel says, rolling his eyes.

"Really?" Nithin says with a happy and excited face.

"Yes, shall we go now?" Neel says happily.

"You two are an unsolved riddle for me. Hahn! I can't understand your friendship," Mithra says with a mock angry face.

Neel put his hand on Nithin's shoulder and smiled.

"Let's go now. You can romance later, and don't do it in front of me. It was unbearable," Mithra teased them.

"Ok, Nithin, if you delay proposing to Manasvi, in the future you will be my boyfriend, not Manasvi's," Neel teased Nithin and hid behind Mithra. Nithin tries to beat him. They all went to the cafe.

4

Aarav and the girl were going in an ambulance to the hospital. "Go to WIOORA Hospital," Aarav says to the ambulance driver, to go to his hospital. "Ok, sir," the driver gave acceptance.

"Shall I ask you some questions?" Aarav asks the boy's girlfriend politely. No response: she was quite thinking something, not aware of Aarav. "Excuse me." Aarav tries to bring her back to reality, so he gives her a double tap on her bag and calls her.

Excuse me, tap on her bag, bring her to the reality of "what happened." Aarav gave her face a miserable smile. "Shall I ask you some questions?" Aarav again asked permission to inquire about her. "Yes, you can," she said, giving him permission with a firm smile.

"What is your name?" I was expecting an answer from her. "My name is Riya," she finally said, opening her mouth.

"Ok, Riya, what is your boyfriend's name?" asks another question. "Harsha," she gave a one-word answer. Aarav understands her state of mind.

"Your boyfriend has a heart problem," Aarav asks her, a practical question.

"No... (Thinking eyes go left and right.) I don't know." First, she says no with a solid voice but stops and takes her time to think after she proclaims she doesn't know with gloomy eyes and a confused reaction.

"Oh, ok, no problem." Aarav was confused. "Why, what happened?" she asks with curiosity. "He had a severe attack on the heart; that's why I'm asking." In a straight line, he answered her question.

She was shocked. "From two weeks ago, he was not right," she gave a suspicious answer. "What? What do you mean is not right; can you explain?" Aarav wants to clear up his confusion by calling it not right. "He was saying something like, 'Leave me; I did not do anything like that, he was saying (with a fearful voice)." It was not clear what happened to her boyfriend.

"What? Something is fishy," Aarav says. He was mulling over. Interrupt: "It was so scary. What this... this... was murder, she says with trembling, and she suddenly leans back with a big breath.

"Yeah! What happens?" Aarav asked with wide-open eyes. She started crying and murmuring. "It's my fault. I should take care of him. I should not leave him like that. When he was saying nonsensical things, I did not contact him, and at that time I was out of the station. Tears flow.

"Anyway, we must give a police complaint, and with the help of a forensic report, we will find what? Is what?" Aarav says with confidence.

"Sir, we reached the hospital," the driver said, breaking their conversation.

They reach the Wioora Hospital, and they get out of the ambulance. The hospital helpers came, and they helped them. They took the stretcher into the hospital and entered the details of the boy.

"What happened, Aarav?" a doctor asks Aarav with fear. "Dr. Vibha, the patient, has died of a heart attack," Aarav answered.

Vibha was a colleague. Aarav had a good friend in her who loved him. She had not yet proposed to him. She was cute and possessive.

"Doctor, is he your relative?" She wants more information. "No, I was at the cafe; there, the boy fell," he said politely, answering her question.

Riya came to Aarav after giving details about Harsha. "Ok, Vibha, this is Riya's patient's girlfriend," he says, introducing her to Vibha. "Ooh" gave a strange expression. "Riya, this is my friend, Dr. Vibha, a cardiologist; she will treat your boyfriend." He gave duty to Vibha. "Ok," Riya says. She looked so painful, and her eyes were filled with tears.

"Ok, come with me (sudden stop). Wait... You did not inform his family?" Vibha asks about Harsha's family. "No, he was an orphan child, and now he was alone," Riya tells Vibha.

"Vibha, what caused the heart attack?" Aarav says to Vibha with duty.

"Riya, if you want something, ask me because Vibha will be busy in the Harsha case."

Aarav's care towards Riya made Vibha angry.

"Don't worry; I will take care. You can go now,"

Vibha said, giving a glare and raising her eyebrows with an angry voice. Aarav gave a smile and moved.

ಲ

In WAN-K NEWS, Manasvi was working as a famous reporter. Her bravery and loyalty were demonstrated in her job. She says what is what. She has naturally brown hair and light grey eyes. She dressed herself in a white shirt and black office suit.

"Madam Fa, we can start the live show in ten minutes," Manasvi says to her boss.

"Manasvi, are you ready for the live show?" Madam Fa asks Manasvi excitedly.

"Yes, ma'am," politely. "Guys, listen, and work correctly; timing is more important, ok?" Manasvi spoke with her team as she was giving instructions.

"Manasvi, listen, this show is going to be sensational, so be careful." Madam Fa was so excited about the show.

Manasvi is now fully prepared for the live show. She sat on the show table, and it was going to start.

"All set, ready to start," the director says loudly to the team. Live started, and all cameras were focusing on Manasvi.

Hello and welcome to WAN-K NEWS.

I'm Manasvi.

Before we begin, I would like to appeal to all to stay safe, especially women, from the serial killer. Yes, so women have weapons with them, like a sharp knife and an electric gun.

Today's topic is: Who? And who?

At almost 6:00 AM, police found the dead body of a woman. The pond was near the road for Ishtan, and there was a corpse. The shocking news is that it was the same killer who has killed two women in the past three months.

But as we know, police arrested a killer three months before and gave him capital punishment. Now the question is, who is the killer? What did the police kill an innocent? Or is someone following his pattern?

The pattern was that first, he tore the neck and then the right side of the cheek. At last, he put paint on the dead body. He was not using the same colors.

In the first murder, he uses yellow paint.

In the second murder, he uses orange paint.

And now he uses green paint.

Video from the site of the murder.

(The video was played from the site of the murder.)

Police are still searching for the killer; it was the third murder.

They don't know who was dead; they don't know any details about the girl.

The police say they will search for the missing case and will find it soon.

We are waiting for more information from the police.

It was the third murder, and the killer was roaming freely in the world, but people are frightened, so we are requesting that the police find the killer soon.

So that's it from us in this Who? And who? But before we leave, I once again appeal to all to stay safe, exclusively women, from the serial killer. Yes, women have weapons with them, like a sharp knife and an electric gun.

We will provide more information as soon as we find it. Thank you for your time.

৪৩

Killer too, watching the live show of Manasvi, the show has ended. "Manasvi, you're so interested in me; one day we are going to meet officially," he says to the television screen with a sarcastic voice.

There was an enormous glass on which he had photos of Kavin, Mithra, Manasvi, Neel, Nithin, Zara, Yamini, Sunaina, and others, too.

He took a red marker and put an X symbol on the photo of Yamini.

5

The clock tower rang eleven bells. Kavin enters the IG office; one constable is waiting outside for him. He went into the conference room. Nithin's father and IG were already in their seats.

"Hello, Kavin, come and take your seat." IG welcomes Kavin.

"Hello, sir," Kavin says with respect, and he takes his seat.

"Mr. Kapil explains," the IG says with a sad face.

"Kavin, you know now what was happening in our Sicilian: the serial killer killed three girls. As you know, it was three months before we arrested a person and gave them capital punishment. But after three months yesterday, the same pattern followed. One girl has been murdered, Nithin's father said woefully, and Kavin nodded his head.

"Yes, sir," Kavin says to Mr. Kapil.

"So, Kavin, now we are going to start an undercover operation, and you are the head of this operation," the IG says to Kavin.

"Thanks for believing me, sir, and I will find him soon," Kavin said with devotion, accepting the case.

"These media are digging the case, and we have to answer their question, so we should be more careful with them," Kapil says with tension and worry.

"Yes, that girl from Wan-K news, her name... Mmmm, Manasvi, she was asking us if we killed innocent people to close this case," IG said, tense and thinking about what to answer.

"Yes, it made me scared," Kapil showed his fear in his face.

"Anyway, we have to face it," Kavin said.

"Police will support you and Mr. Kapil in the operation," the IG says.

"Sir, can you explain the case details?" Kavin asks Kapil.

"Yes, but first we have to go to the undercover operation place," Mr. Kapil says, taking the case file to explain.

"Ohh! Yes, we can," Kavin says. He was excited about the case.

"Sir, shall we move now?" Kapil asks permission from the IG.

"Yes, Mr. Kapil, you can," the IG permitted them.

"Thank you, sir," Kavin and Kapil say to IG. They got up and moved from their chairs. Suddenly, IG calls them and says, "All the best," with a firm smile. "Grab him and don't leave him," with a furious voice and wide-open eyes.

"Yes, sir," they say in a loud voice with respect.

They came from the IG office.

They came to their cars.

"Kavin, direct back to the IG office, and there was an old building; that's our place. Shall we go now?" Kapil gives the location to Kavin.

"Ok, sir," Kavin says while nodding his head.

"Follow my car," Kapil says, and he takes it.

Kavin drove his car, and he followed Kapil's car. They went to an old building, and they entered the building.

∞

The building was old from the outside. Inside, there is a secure iron door with a password. Kapil opened the door with his password and fingerprint.

"How much security?" Kavin says it with a shocking reaction. Kapil smiled at Kavin.

Kapil set Kavin's fingerprint and told him the password, too.

They came inside. There were advanced computers, CCTV, a cupboard, etc., the things that were necessary for them. There were four officers involved in the operation.

They introduce themselves as "Am Smith, Am Yuan, Am Sultan, and Am Rahul." They say it with an inflexible chest and a bold voice.

"Ok, Am Kavin," in his style.

"Yeah, we know," Yuan says with a smile.

"Kavin is our head in this operation," Kapil informs them.

"Ok, officer, shall we begin this undercover operation?" Kavin says it with excited eyes.

"Yes," they say, and they take their seat at the round table.

Kapil took some photos, forensic reports, and some documents. He shows a group photo.

"Kavin, see this photo; there are four members in this group photo. They are friends, and their names are Aksana, Shefali, Yamini, and Sunaina. Aksana and Shefali were murdered three months ago, and yesterday Yamini was murdered. Kapil explained the case to him.

"Sir Sunaina," Kavin asks, his doubt.

"Sunaina had a terrible accident last night, and now she was admitted to Wioora Hospital," Kapil cleared his doubt. "Yesterday she was supposed to give a missing complaint about Yamini; on the way to the police station, a broken truck caused an accident," Kapil added, adding more information about Sunaina.

"In Wioora Hospital?" Kavin asks with curious eyes.

"Yes, why?" Kapil asks with confusion.

"No sir. So, now Sunaina was in danger. We must save her and arrest the killer soon," Kavin says with red eyes. The eyes show how much he was interested.

"Sir, show me the forensic reports and case file," Kavin asks Kapil. Kapil showed the reports. Kavin analyzes both reports.

"Sir, all reports match," Kavin says with confusion.

"Yes, Kavin, he follows the same pattern and date, too." Kapil simply declares this.

"Sir, they died at the same age of twenty-six, and the date is six," Kavin says with wide-open eyes.

"Kavin, see Sunaina's age," Kapil says with shock. Rahul opens Sunaina's file, and they check her age. It was twenty-five soon, and they checked her date of birth. They became shocked and speechless.

"November six, next month," Sultan says with wide-open eyes.

They all saw each other.

"Ok, first we didn't know when the murder was going to happen, but now we know when it is going to happen," Kapil said with positivity.

"We have to watch Sunaina; somehow he will come to meet her," Rahul says with confidence.

"We have to inquire about her, and before the media finds her, we have to change her place," Kavin says.

"Ok, I and Rahul will go to the hospital; Smith will search for the fake killer; and Sultan will go to Yamini's home and search for a clue." Kavin allotted their work.

"Me?" Yuan asks Kavin with raised eyebrows and a smile.

"Mr. Kapil and you will search in the CCTV footage, okay?" Kavin says with a smile.

They are ready to do their duty and have moved from their place. Kavin turned to the wall and saw the calendar hanging on the wall. He sprightly moved to the calendar and took it.

"We have an extra calendar," Kavin asks.

"Yes, we have," Kapil says. All are confused and watching Kavin.

Kavin turned the page and took the marker. He circled on November 6. All went to do their duty.

୫

Meanwhile, the killer was looking at Sunaina's photo and took a red marker from his table. He circled Sunaina in her photo, and there was a group photo of the Kavin team.

There is one difference: the killer has a group photo with five members: four girls and one boy. But the Kavin team has a group photo with four members. A boy was missing in the photo.

Killer played the song *I Can See You (a song by Taylor Swift and Nicholas Brodszky)*. He vibes with the song, and he moves to the calendar that is hanging on the wall. He turns the page of the calendar and hangs it on the wall. He took the same red marker and circled the date, November 6.

6

Killer's phone pops up the message. He took his phone and checked.

The message is: check the camera recorder.

He saw a camera on the table and off his phone. He took the camera and played the recorder. Then it played, and he started watching it.

In that, there was Yamini. She crosses the road, and she is not conscious of the vehicles. One black car is coming at high speed. The car gives horns. She was not aware and was thinking about something.

On the roadside, the members are shouting, and Yamini comes back to consciousness of what's occurring around her. The car came near and put on a sudden brake. Yamini says sorry to the person in the car. The roadside members are seeing Yamini.

There was a cake shop; she went to the cake shop.

⇛

In the cake shop:

There was a sales attendant. Yamini asked to give the butterscotch cake, which was ordered this morning.

"Mam, your name, please," the sales boy asked Yamini. She gave her name. The seller checks the order on the system. Yamini was waiting for the cake.

"Yes, ma'am, you ordered today at 11:30," he says with a smile.

"Yes," Yamini says. The sales attendant brings the cake. Yamini saw the cake; it had a strawberry flavor.

"My order was butterscotch cake, not strawberry," she says with tension.

"Sorry, ma'am, we made a mistake," the sales boy says politely.

"Look, my order was butterscotch, so give butterscotch," she says angrily.

"Mam, we finish icing; we can't do anything," he politely refuses to take back.

"Ok, give me a strawberry cake, but you should give it to me for free," she says with raised eyebrows.

"Ma'am, I did not make the mistake," he said, shocked by Yamini's words.

Yamini went to the cash counter. The cake shop owner was sitting. She says the mistake was in the cake. The owner called the seller boy and told him to make the butterscotch cake.

"Mam, please wait," the owner says, telling Yamini to wait.

Yamini was waiting on the chair and thinking about something. The seller boy came there, and he called Yamini. But she did not respond to the boy. The boy tapped Yamini's hand. She got back to her senses and asked, "What?"

"Mam, the cake has been ready," the boy says. "Ok, give," she says.

"Mam, pay cash at the cash counter," the boy says.

"I know what to do and what not to do. Go and do your work properly. Move from here." She says it harshly.

The boy moved and put his head down. She went to the cash counter. She gave cash to the cashier. The cashier took her cash and said, "Ma'am, sorry for our mistake, and we will make you wait."

"Teach your employees to do the work properly," she says with attitude.

"My employee apologized to you and was polite to you, but what did you do? Is that correct?" The cashier says.

Yamini got annoyed and asked, "What?"

"You have to say sorry." The cashier says.

She smirked. "To whom?"

The cashier calls the seller boy and tells her to ask for forgiveness.

"If I refuse to ask, sorry, what will you do?" She says it with a raised eyebrow.

"I will file a complaint against you." The cashier shows CCTV, and he warns her. Yamini asks, "Sorry."

ಜ

Outside the cake shop:

Yamini came out of the shop and murmured, "Who found this CCTV?"

She crosses the road, waits for the bus, and looks upset. She was standing at the bus stop, and there was a jewelry shop. She was looking at that jewelry, and a person was looking towards Yamini. She notices him. He is coming near her. She is murmuring, "Here should be the CCTV."

The bus came, and she got on the bus. She is sitting in the seat. The person also got on the bus and came near Yamini. Yamini is standing behind the cone lady. The lady understands Yamini's problem. The bus was going; the lady gave him a stare.

"What do you want to go to prison?" the lady asks, angry.

The man went from there. Yamini, thank that lady. She talks nicely with Yamini. Yamini thinks, "One good thing that happened means it's meeting this lady." The lady stopped came; she got off the bus and said goodbye to Yamini. Yamini is alone and going home.

(As we know, the killer followed Yamini and took her into his car.)

7

The killer came to his place, and there is a basement. He took Yamini to the basement and put her down. He ties her hand and leg so that she cannot run. After a while, she became conscious. The killer saw her, and she became conscious. There was a fire gun; he took it and heated the iron road in front of Yamini. She was scared, and she begged him to leave her alive. He started heating it. It's becoming red. He got up, and there was a blackboard he brought towards Yamini. He is writing on the blackboard instead of talking.

"Why do you want to spoil the project, CB?" He asks Yamini.

Yamini asks, "Who are you? Why are you doing this?" with tears.

"What do you want to die of soon?" The killer writes.

Yamini was crying, and he came near her. It was highly heated. Yamini says, "Please don't do this. I will tell you what happened." She started talking about the past few days.

Seven days before:

Yamini was working at Lovely Cosmetics. Mithra came there, and she was selecting a member for a new project launch, which is

CB. She selects Yamini and some other bits, not Sunaina.

The project CB is Mithra's dream project, and it is her aim. The project CB (Cherry Blossom) is a waterproof cream with a cherry blossom flower. The flower was dried and then powdered. After that, add chemicals and natural things. The CB cream was good for the skin, and it suits all skin types, especially sensitive skin. We can hide our scars on the face with the help of CB. The work is going seriously, and all are working hard for this project.

The next day, Yamini was getting ready to go to the company by the time a heavy fever affected her mom. So, she took her mom to the hospital. Doctors say that she is affected by fourth-stage cancer.

"Why did you hide this from me, mom?" She was shocked, and she asked her with tears.

Her mom says she doesn't want to make Yamini worry. Yamini was crying and asking doctors to treat her.

"We cannot do anything. Sorry to say, but it is the reality that you must accept. Fulfill your mom's wishes and take care of her," the doctor says to Yamini with sadness.

౪౦

Then I came home:

After this, they came home. She took leave without informing the company. She takes care of her mom.

"Mom, till my breath, I will protect you." Yamini was crying and spoke.

"Yamini, can you take me to an amusement park?" Yamini's mom asks for her last wish.

Yamini makes a promise that she will take her day off tomorrow.

After the day, she went to the company. Mithra came to Yamini.

"What, Yamini, did you forget now that you are working on my project? Say, why did you take leave without informing me?" Mithra asks Yamini. Yamini tries to explain her mom's health. But she was not willing to listen for any reason.

"The CB project will be launched very soon, so be careful and work for the project," Mithra says, with anger.

Yamini says nothing. After lunch, "Shall I take leave tomorrow?" Yamini asks Mithra.

Mithra was angry and said not to leave. She gave Yamini a lot of work and told her to do it.

Yamini was angry and wanted to do something. She is talking with Sunaina about her mom's health. Sunaina tries to console Yamini.

Yamini came home after her work, and she saw that, in her usual way, the construction work started, so she must go another way. But the way is dark and horrible. She went home that way.

Her mom was cooking for Yamini. She saw that her mom was cooking, and she got angry. She snatches the ladle. She cooks for her mom.

After cooking, she became tired. She took a bath and came to eat dinner. They are both eating their dinner.

ೞ

The next day, she woke up and woke her mom. They are getting ready to go to an amusement park. Yamini's mom was happy, and by seeing her, Yamini felt happy. She was not thinking about her job. She wants to make her mom happy and wants to take care of her. They are going to the park by bus. They went to an amusement park, and she bought a ticket.

They went inside the park and looked at her mom. Yamini's mom was happy, like a child. Looking at her, Yamini was crying.

"What do you want to eat?" Yamini asks her mom.

"Shall we sit on a Ferris wheel?" Yamini's mom says.

"Of course, Mom, ask me anything else if you want," Yamini says.

They both sat on a Ferris wheel, and her mom was enjoying herself so much. They were both very happy. Suddenly, Yamini's mom takes a bloody breath. Yamini wipes her mouth. Yamini's mom wants to go on the carousel. Yamini takes her to the carousel. They went on another riddled rollercoaster, a big pendulum, a flying chair, and a pirate ship.

They eat lots of food. Cotton candy, funnel cake, popcorn, corn dogs, hot dogs, garlic fries, ice cream, burgers, pizza, and her favorite butterscotch cake.

They went to a 3D show, and they spent the day happily. At last, they went to a movie after watching a movie. They went to a luxurious restaurant. There, they eat luxurious food. They hate cuisine. They went for a candlelight dinner. Yamini fulfills her mom's wish.

They came home by cab. After coming home, Yamini's mom vomited blood. Yamini and her mom take a bath. Yamini checks her wallet; it's empty.

"Yamini, you spent lots of money today, so, for you, there is one thing." Yamini's mom calls Yamini and tells.

"What is that, mom?" Yamini asks

"Yamini, for your marriage, I saved some money, and now I am thinking that I do not have many days in my life and am not lucky." Yamini's mom tells.

"Mom, please don't talk like this; it's hurting me so much," Yamini says.

"Yamini, use this money for your marriage." Yamini's mom gave her an account book to Yamini. Yamini hugs her mom and cries.

They are talking happily about today's enjoyment and seeing today's photos. They are sleeping together.

8

The next day, Yamini got ready to go to the company and made breakfast. They eat breakfast, and she prepares lunch for her and her mom. She packed her lunch and went to her office. In the office, all are working seriously. Yamini came to her table.

"Why did you come to work?" Mithra came near Yamini and asked,

"Sorry, my mom is sick; that's why I took leave," Yamini says

"Ooh! She is fine," Mithra says.

Yamini was standing with watery eyes. Mithra went from there. Yamini started doing her work. Sunaina asks Yamini about her mom's health.

"Mom becomes weaker day by day," Yamini says, crying and worrying about her mom's health.

After finishing work, Yamini and Sunaina went to the club. In the club, they drink, and Yamini is not in her hand. She drank heavily. Sunaina calls her boyfriend to come to the club. Sunaina's boyfriend came to the club. He asks, "What happened? Sunaina, are you okay?" Sunaina and her boyfriend took Yamini. Sunaina's boyfriend has a car. Sunaina took Yamini's hand and put it on her shoulder. In her boyfriend's car, Sunaina brought Yamini to her home.

They reach Yamini's home and knock on the door. Yamini's mom opens the door, and her daughter is like this.

"Ooh! Come in, Sunaina. What happened to her? Why is she like this?" She was scared and asked

"Mom, nothing to worry about; she drank," Sunaina says.

Yamini's mom tells Sunaina to take her to her bedroom. After letting Yamini go to bed, they came out of the room. Sunaina and her boyfriend sat on the sofa.

"Why is she drinking that much?" Yamini's mom says.

"Don't worry, Mom, she will be fine," Sunaina says.

"Sunaina, who is this guy?" Yamini's mom asks

"Mom, he is my boyfriend," Sunaina says.

"Hello, my name is Akash. Nice to meet you." Sunaina's boyfriend Yamini's mom was happy to see Akash's respect.

"Mom, how is your health?" Sunaina says

"Not bad, Sunaina; please take care of her posthumously." Yamini's mom says

her words shocked "Mom, please, don't talk like this," she says with tears.

"Sunaina, you are the only person for Yamini to take good care of her and take care of yourself." Yamini's mom burst into tears and said,

"Mom, I do not have a mother to take care of like you are taking care of Yamini, and I saw you like my mom; you also treat me as you treat Yamini," Sunaina says.

"Sunaina, you are my unborn daughter, and your mom and I are good friends." Yamini's mom says.

Sunaina and her boyfriend want to go.

"Mom, it's getting late; we have to go," Sunaina says

"Okay, go safe and be careful while driving," Yamini's mom says.

"Mom, please take care of yourself, and Mom, give this hangover medicine to Yamini." Sunaina hugs Yamini's mom and says,

"Ok, bye." Yamini's mom says

Akash says bye to Yamini's mom, Sunaina, and Akash and Sunaina both go from Yamini's home. Yamini's mom locked the door, switched off the lights, and went to the room. She and Yamini sleep well.

৪৩

Tomorrow morning, Yamini got up late with a headache. Yamini's mom made breakfast and lunch for Yamini. Yamini was frustrated with herself. She gave that medicine, which was given by Sunaina last night. Yamini got up and ate breakfast. She took the medicine and was ready to go to the office. Her mom sends her a message and says, "Yamini, be careful." Yamini went from her home and reached the bus stop. The bus came, and she got on the bus. The bus started in a few minutes, but there was heavy traffic. She is angry and prays to God. After the traffic cleared, the bus went, and she thanked God. The bus reaches Yamini's spot. She runs into the office faster than the lightning. But it became late.

Mithra is sitting at her table when she does this. Yamini was struck dumb. Mithra saw Yamini and told her, "Madam, come in. Why are you standing outside? Madam, why are you sweating? Ahh! What do you break mountain?" with sarcasm. Mithra shouted at Yamini in front of everyone and removed her from the CB project. It was a shameful moment for Yamini.

Yamini planned to combine chemical sulfates, which are harmful to the skin. Yamini entered the research room. The sample products are stored, and she mixes the chemicals.

ೞ

The next day, sample products were tested, but the results were good.
The project was a success; Yamini was shocked.

"What happened, Yamini?" Mithra asks Yamini.

Yamini and Sunaina are both standing nervously. Mithra came near Yamini. Yamini was shocked and looked at Mithra. Mithra came angrily and slapped Yamini's face. Yamini is stunned.

"We bend over backward for this project, CB (Cherry Blossom)," Mithra says.

"Yamini, you are fired." The chairperson came there and told.

"Why? What did I do?" Yamini was angry and asked,

Mithra showed her phone the recorded video. In that video, Yamini enters the research room and opens the chemical box. Adding some things to that. It is recorded.

Mithra says, "What are you thinking, Yamini? When did she keep the camera? Or why did she not tell me this before? Mithra says, "One shall be punished for their evil deeds."

Yamini was furious and said, "Mithra, you will face consequences, and the project CB will be destroyed."

"The CB product is my dream project; if something happens to it, you will die in my hand." Mithra shouted at Yamini, "Are you understanding?"

"Ok." Yamini smirks.

"Get out of here, or I will kill you," Mithra says.

Sunaina came to say something, but Yamini held her hand, and she said no by nodding her head. The other members are controlling Mithra.

"Mithra, be calm. We will inform the police that she added chemical sulfates. The chairperson says:

"No, sir, she has to see the success of CB," Mithra says.

"Ok, Yamini, it is time to get out of the company," Mithra tells Yamini.

"Ok, all is well. Go and do your work." The chairperson says:

All the members went to their places, but Mithra stood there and looked at Yamini. Yamini went to her table and started packing her things. She gave Mithra a stare. Mithra and the other company members are also looking at Yamini. The members murmured about Yamini. Yamini was frustrated, and Sunaina helped pack her things." They finish packing, and Yamini gets out of the office. Sunaina helps Yamini carry her things, but.

Yamini leaves her job and goes to the beach. She switched off the phone, and she spent much time after she realized it was getting dark. "Ooh! I must leave," and she came to the cake shop.

౭౦

(She ends the flashback, as we know what happened at the cake shop.)

"I told everything now. Please leave me. I want to take care of my mom. She has only a few days. Please let me go. I won't complain about you, and I won't tell anyone about this. Please leave me alive." Yamini was constantly begging for life. She was crying hard.

The killer took a knife and came near Yamini, and he grabbed her head forcefully. She looked scared at her. "Please." The killer tore her cheek. The blood dripped down. Yamini screamed and cried.

"I know Mithra told you to do this; please leave me. I will not disturb her, and I will leave Sisalian," she begs with tears and pain in her voice.

"It's too late," the killer wrote on the board. He took the knife and neared Yamini.

"Leave my mom." She understood what was going to happen; she understood that he would leave her by killing her, so she asked her mom to leave.

The killer cut her neck; she was trembling; the blood was bleeding; she died there. When he came close to the camera, he made some hand signals and showed green paint. The recorder ends here.

9

Kavin and Rahul went to the hospital; they asked the receptionist about Sunaina, and they went to the ward. Sunaina was watching the news about Yamini's death; actually, she was crying. Kavin and Rahul went near Sunaina. She then asks, "Who are you?"

"We are police," Rahul said, showing his identification card.

"There is no use for you to be here; it's too late. My friend died; she will kill me also," Sunaina says with tears and hopelessness.

"She, what you mean, you know, is the killer," Kavin asks with confusion.

"She is Mithra; she only killed all my friends, and now she will kill me too," Sunaina says with true eyes.

"Mithra, who is she?" Kavin asks, accepting the answer.

"It's your girlfriend," Sunaina said confidently.

"What? Do you know what you're saying? Kavin looks angry.

"Same; no one believed us and arrested someone; now she killed my friend," she cries with guilt.

"How can you be so confident? Do you have any proof?" Rahul asks.

"I don't have any proof against her that she was roaming freely," Sunaina said with anger.

"Then how do you say that she is the killer?" Kavin says with a raised eyebrow.

"She says that" she said, starting to cry.

"What did she say?" Kavin asks with curiosity.

"That that... She will kill everyone." Sunaina says, but seems suspicious in a word.

"When?" Kavin asked silently.

"On Aksana's engagement," Sunaina says with woefulness.

"Can you explain what happened?" Rahul asks with wide eyes.

౷

Two years ago, Lyziden Aksana and Advik got engaged grandly. There is lots of food, and the decorations are massive. There are relatives busy with gossip and friends busy roasting each other. Aksana, Shefali, Yamini, and Sunaina are all happily taking photos there until Mithra appears. Aksana looks scared.

"Wow, your engagement is grand, and you all look happy," Mithra says with a sarcastic smile on her face.

"Why did you come here? We did not even invite you." Aksana was angry and looked scared.

"To see your last smiling faces," Mithra says with the same attitude.

"Aksana, why is she here? Did you invite her?" Advik says it with tenacity.

"No, why should I call her?" Aksana clarified her doubt.

"Hey. Get out of here," Advik and Shefali Attar said at the same time.

"I don't want to be here. Just goodbye. You all will face the tragedy soon." Mithra had tensed eyes, and she went from there.

Aksana's marriage was going to happen after two months, and every arrangement was going well. The one call changed everything; it was from Advik's mom. She says that Advik attempted suicide. We went there, and he fell down the stairs. It is an apartment on fifty floors.

Aksana went into depression, and after six months, we all went on our paths. The news came that Aksana had been murdered and Shefali had been murdered. We understand someone is targeting us. I and Yamini joined Lovely Cosmetics when we met Mithra.

Mithra tortured us in every single way, and now Yamini is murdered. I am sure she will kill me; definitely, no one will save me. Got emotional and started sobbing.

Suddenly, she went unconscious while talking.

"Sunaina, what happened? DOCTOR. DOCTOR." Rahul shouted, and the doctors came there.

"She is stressed; don't disturb her." Doctors check her.

Kavin and Rahul came out of the room. Rahul noted that Kavin was silent and deep in thought.

"Sir, what happened?" Rahul asks with sad eyes.

"We have inquired, Mithra," with commanding eyes.

"Ok, sir," Rahul accepted.

They moved from there and went to the ground floor.

"Kavin... Kavin.., stop." Aarav came by, running. I caught Kavin and took a breath. "Several times I called you; what are you doing here?" he asks.

"Casework." Kavin gave a short answer.

"Do you remember the morning one person got stroked at the cafe?" Aarav tried to convey something about the morning incident.

"Yes, I remember what happened to him." Kavin accepted the answer with curiosity.

"He died, but something is suspicious, according to which I want to talk." Aarav wants help from Kavin.

"Ok, but now I am on the big case; we will talk later," Kavin says.

"Ok, Kavin, bye." understand the situation.

They came out of the hospital.

&

"First, we have to go to our place," Kavin says to Rahul with a flat face.

"Ok, sir," Rahul says, and when they take their car from the parking area, he brings the car, and Kavin is silent, not aware of what is happening around him.

"Sir," Rahul calls him, but there is no response. "Sir" again.

"Oh, yes." He came to reality and got into the car.

Rahul drove the car to a secret place. They went from there, and the deep silence took place on Kavin.

10

Sultan went to Yamini's home. He too went the long way because of that construction work. He found a phone. He took that and put it on the cover. When he reached Yamini's home, he saw a cake at the entrance. He took photos and saw the cake was messed up. He noted down the cake shop address and took photos. He went inside the house, and he searched for someone. No, their house was silent. Their photos hung on the wall. There was a photo of Yamini and her mom. Also, there were a friend's photos, and he saw a group photo that was the same as the one the killer has. He took photos and took that group photo from Yamini's home. He searched, but nothing was there, so he decided to go to the cake shop.

∞

He went to the cake shop.

"Do you know this is where she came here?" Sultan shows his ID proof and asks about Yamini by showing her photo.

"Yes, sir, yesterday she brought a cake from here," the owner says with confusion.

"Yesterday... (After some silence) Can I check the CCTV?" Sultan asks for permission.

"Sure, sir." The owner showed the CCTV recorders of yesterday.

The record had played. Sultan watched carefully; he observed how she behaved and watched outside the camera. He saw the red car waiting for Yamini till she came outside. He copied the recorders into a pen drive, and he decided to go to the secret place.

೮೦

"Where is Smith till he doesn't come?" Kapil asks surprisingly.

"I will call him," Yuan says to Kapil.

Someone was opening the door; everyone saw on the telegram it was Smith. "Finally he came. Let's start the discussion," Yuan says.

Smith looking at everyone's face. "What happened? Why are you staring at everyone like this?" Rahul asks with curious eyes.

"Nothing, I'm just confused," Smith finally makes a talk.

"What... You went to search for that previous killer, right? Tell me what happened. Kapil says.

"There is less information about that killer. The killer's name is Mahit. He was an orphan who grew up at Zara Orphanage. It is in Lyziden, and when he turned twenty, he left the orphanage. He was in a relationship with the owner's daughter; after that, the girl attempted suicide. After that, only he killed Aksana and Shefali. This much information I only got from records. So, I searched more with the help of my friend." Silence took place. Everyone was looking at Smith.

"My friend was working in Lyziden, so I asked for help from him. I told him to seek information from the orphanage. He entered there as Mahit's friend, and he collected some information. He also sent some photos to me," Smith shows photos.

"The original owner of Zara Orphanage died nine years ago; after that, the owner's brother undertook the orphanage and his brother's daughter. The brother took care of the child and the orphanage. Zara was the name of the original owner's daughter. The girl the killer loved was the brother's daughter. Three years ago she committed suicide. Her name was. Zoya, after this, Zara and the brother did not come to the orphanage. There was Aunty Jo, who is taking care of the orphanage under Zara's control."

"How did they give this much information to anyone?" Rahul asks with shock.

"He collects this much information from a girl. He can make any girl fall for him. He is a playboy," Smith says with a jealous smirk.

"Why do you look so jealous?" Yuan asks. "My girlfriend also fell for him," Smith says, with blinking eyes. Everyone laughed at Smith's answer.

"OK, enough. I am coming to the point." Smith avoided them and started explaining again.

"Here it is, a group photo taken fifteen years ago. There is a photo of the original owner of the orphanage, and there is a photo of Zoya," Smith shows photos.

"After Zoya's death, Mahit never comes to the orphanage, and they never know that Mahit was the killer who was arrested three months before. We don't know where he went when he was twenty years old because in the record it only mentions the orphanage name; there is nothing," Smith says with sadness.

"How did you arrest him and give capital punishment too, also not having proper information about him?" Kavin asks Kapil.

ॐ

What does what happened mean?

After Aksana's death, we search for the killer, but to no avail, and no murder has happened. But once we got Shefali's missing complaint, we were in search of CCTV. We saw a minivan that followed Shefali, and we found where the car went, so we went to that place. We saw a car that was stuck in the mud on the street, and it looked like the same car, so we got out of our car and went to see it. Suddenly the car driver ran from the car. It was Mahit, me, and another policeman. We both ran behind him. We caught him in a blocked street, and one call came to me from a policeman who came with us. I attended the call. He said that in that car there was blood and a lady's scarf. So we arrested him and took him to prison.

We sent that blood sample to the forensic department. The next day we got Shefali's dead body with the same pattern that followed in Aksana's case. Shefali posted her picture in the morning, in which she wore a scarf that was the scarf only found in that car.

After that, the forensic report of the blood we collected from it came. It mentions that there are three DNA samples: one is male and two are female. We came to know that the male DNA matches with Mahit, and the two females are Aksana and Shefali.

He doesn't open his mouth. We beat him then to never say a word. We forcefully open his mouth. We are shocked. He has no tongue; it has been cut in half. But all the evidence was against him.

He was an orphan. He grew up in Zara orphanage, and he left there when he was born. Twenty after that, he was in a relationship with Zoya, the daughter of the orphanage owner. Zoya committed suicide. So with this, we concluded that because of his girlfriend's death, he became a serial killer.

We submitted the case in court. He accepted everything and was given capital punishment.

We closed this case, but we alerted Yamini and Sunaina also to be careful; everything was till yesterday, but the murder happened with the same pattern.

৪৩

"How do you guess Yamini and Sunaina will get a problem?" Kavin asks Kapil.

"We found a group photo from Shefali's home, so we guess next they will get a problem, but as we gave capital punishment to Mahit, we just alert them to be careful," Kapil answered.

"You alerted Yamini and Sunaina, so why did you not alert Shefali?" Yuan asks.

"When he killed Aksana, we didn't know anything about the killer. There was no clue, and nothing was. Suspicious by seeing the pattern of murder, we guessed it would be a serial killer. That's it. After he killed Shefali, we got a group photo, so we came to know Aksana and Shefali were friends. In that, there were Yamini and Sunaina, so we alerted them. But we followed them for one month; everything was ok, so we let it." Kapil says.

"What, one month?" Rahul was shocked.

"Yes, because he killed Shefali after one month; that's why," Kapil cleared everyone's doubt.

"I have seen him somewhere," Sultan says.

"Where?" Smith asks

"Yes, morning, Mr Kapil, show his photo," Rahul remembers

"No, somewhere I saw... (After deep thinking) Ooh yes, in Yamini's home," Sultan remembers.

"What in Yamini's home?" Rahul and Smith are in the chorus.

11

Sultan's eyes were fixed on the group as he revealed the photographs he had taken from Yamini's home. The air was thick with anticipation, and the images captured everyone's attention.

"Is this the boy you were referring to?" Rahul asked, his face was confusing.

"But he doesn't look like Mahit." Sultan's gaze remained steady.

"No, not him. Look closely behind him. Mahit is there."

The group's collective focus shifted, scanning the photograph until they found Mahit's face. Smith's voice trembled with shock. "Yes, he's there."

The room fell into silence as the weight of the discovery sank in. Kavin broke the stillness. "It seems that Mahit was involved in the murder." Yuan narrowed his eyes.

"What about the girl standing next to him? Her face is unclear." Sultan's expression turned grim. "I couldn't capture a clear shot of her face."

The group's attention turned back to the photograph, their minds racing with possibilities.

It was Smith who broke the silence, his voice barely audible. "Aksana was dressed like a bride in this photo. And look, there's a groom beside her." Rahul's eyes widened in surprise.

"So, Aksana was engaged?" Kapil's voice grew sombre. "Yes, but the engagement was called off. Her fiancé, Advik, committed suicide."

Once again, the room fell into silence as the group processed this new information. Smith's voice carried scepticism. "What if Advik's death wasn't a suicide?"

"Where it happened?" Kavin asks.

"In Lyziden," Kapil says.

"Ahhh! Everything is connecting with Lyziden," Rahul says with stress.

Kavin's eyes locked onto the Sultan. "Did you find anything else at Yamini's home?" Sultan's expression remained unchanged.

"When I went to her street, I got one cell phone, and at the entrance of her house, there was a cake," Sultan showed the phone and the cake photo.

"I went inside her house; there only I collected these photos, and there was no one in the house, so I came from there. I went to that cake shop," Sultan says what happened in the cake shop, and he showed a CCTV recorder of the cake shop.

"I watch the outside camera of the shop there. I notice one red car follows Yamini," Sultan says about the killer's car.

"Yes, the red car we saw on CCTV follows Yamini. But when it entered the street, it disappeared. I think it must be the killer's car," Kapil says.

"After that, no camera did catch him," Yuan added.

Yuan's voice was laced with determination. "We need to investigate further. What happened to Sunaina?"

Kavin was silent. Rahul saw Kavin being quiet and made him explain what happened there. Rahul explained everything. But he stops hesitating to talk about Mithra. Rahul silently looked at Kavin.

"She doubts Mithra," Kavin says.

"Mithra, who is she?" Smith asks

"Mithra? You mean our Mithra?" Kapil asks with confusion.

"Yes," Kavin gave one word.

"Can anybody tell me who she is?" Smith says.

"My girlfriend," Kavin says with a flat face.

Everyone was shocked, and silence took place. All eyes are on Kavin, waiting for an explanation. Finally, Kavin started explaining everything.

"Why will Mithra kill them?" Kapil asks

"While talking, she went unconscious. We came," Rahul says.

"That means Mithra also went to Aksana's engagement," Smith asks.

"Yes," Rahul nods his head.

"Kavin, do you have any idea that she went there?" Sultan asks

"Yes, but she constantly goes to her native place," Kavin says.

"What is her native place?" Smith asks.

"Lyziden," Kavin says with fearful eyes. Everyone looks shocked.

"How will we confirm that Mithra went there?" Kapil asks

"Can you show me all the photos that you have taken from Yamini's home?" Kavin says

"See, here it is." Sultan shows all the photos. Everyone carefully searches for every photo.

"I found," Smith shouts.

"What have you found?" Rahul asks.

"That girl," Smith says with a proud smile.

"What?" Rahul was confused.

"That girl who was talking with the killer on her face is clear in this photo," Smith said, and he showed a photo of Yamini and Sunaina. "Behind Yamini, she was there," Smith added.

"Yes, look at her. She is a little clear about this," Rahul says with surprise.

Everyone looking at that photo, "Show me," Kavin asks. They pass to Kavin.

Kavin looks shocked, wide-eyed. "It's Mithra," he says.

"Let me see," Kapil asks. Rahul gave it to Kapil. After seeing it, he kept silent. Everyone was looking at Kapil, so he nodded his head and said yes. Staring at each other silently.

"Kavin, can you show us Mithra's photo?" Sultan asks. After some silence, Kavin shows Mithra's photo on his phone. They saw Mithra's photo and confirmed it.

"That means the girl who was talking with Mahit is Mithra," Yuan says.

"What do we have to do now?" Smith asks while seeing Kavin.

"We must investigate... (After some silence)... We have to investigate Mithra.

<h1 style="text-align:center">12</h1>

"Aarav!" Vibha calls, no, she shouts his name.

"What happened? Why are you shouting?" Aarav asks with confusion.

"I want to talk with you," Vibha says, keeping eye contact.

"OK, say what happened," Aarav asks to avoid eye contact.

"Not here," Vibha says with a firm smile.

"Then where," he asks, having no idea what she is talking about.

"To my room," Vibha says casually.

"What!!!" Aarav was by her answer.

"I am talking about my cabin," Vibha ends his thoughts.

"Ooh!" He gave a relaxed smile.

"Come, it's a serious one about that patient," Vibha says, what she wants to talk about.

They both go to Vibha's cabin. Riya was sitting outside the cabin. It was Vibha and Aarav coming there. Aarav saw her. "Riya, come. Vibha wants to talk about your boyfriend's case only." Aarav joined Riya too.

"Hey, what are you doing?" Vibha asks Aarav with confusion.

"Why, what happened?" Aarav has no idea.

"Aarav, we are doctors. First, we must talk; after that only, we have to convey anything to the attendant," Vibha says. The tense voice scares Aarav and makes him say, "Ok.".

"Ok, no problem. I will wait to hear," Riya says.

They both went inside the cabin. "Why behave rudely to her?" Aarav asks casually.

"I feel something is wrong. She talks with you, and the way she sees you—AHH, I feel some negative vibes. Vibha is trying to hide her jealous feelings.

"What are you saying? Now she is brokenhearted," still having no idea of her feelings.

"She was hiding something." The irritation on her face says everything.

"I don't feel wrong with her. I feel wrong with this case," says the innocent face.

"You are right; see this." She understood he wouldn't understand, so she came back to professional mode.

Vibha took some documents and photos. "See, this is Harsha's report," she gave to him.

He was reading the report, looking serious and looking handsome. The eyes moving here and there look like a fish in water. The nose was sharp, and the lips were tempting to kiss. The sweat touching his cheeks and the expression on his face for the report made him more handsome. Why is he so hot? The veins in his hands were green-blue, making him blush. Because of the flash of light, making his eyes brown. Vibha admires him with unblinking eyes and an uncontrollable smile. Aarav saw her. I think he felt her. The eyes met the beats; the smile stopped. It made him forget the place, the surroundings, the gender, the emotion, the world, everything. That one blink of Aarav changed everything.

Whatever the eye contact moment making the butterfly means, after an embarrassing moment, it makes it sour and sweet. Suddenly remembering everything that I forgot at that moment makes it hard to manage.

"What you saw was everything Ewe!!! I mean, you read everything?" She, with embarrassed eyes, did not dare to make another eye contact.

"Yeah. Yes... Yes, I read. At last, he felt something.

"Here you have mentioned some poison. I don't understand that," Aarav asks with doubt. Now the procession has taken place.

"It is cyanide poison. It is only used for gold, and it is harmful to human health," Vibha says.

"It used to polish gold after that. I don't know anything about that," he cleared his doubt.

"Yes," she says with dutiful eyes.

"Then how did it come into his body?" He was confused.

"Last he drank coffee in that this poison was mixed," Vibha says.

"What does it mean? He intentionally takes that poison," Aarav says with shock.

"Yes, it was intentionally taken or given," Vibha says. Aarav has deep thoughts while being silent.

"It could be suicide or else murder," he concluded.

"Yes, I am sure it is not a natural death," she finished it.

"Ok, then I will inform you of this, Riya. After that, we go for the police," Aarav decided.

"But Aarav, before that, we have to inform you about this to the head," Vibha says. She looks confused.

"Vibha, you go and inform your head, ok, before we talk to Riya," Aarav says.

"Ok, I will call her." Vibha went to call Riya.

They call Riya inside the cabin. She came, and Aarav told her everything. She was shocked and became blank.

"Now what should I do?" Riya asks with fear.

"Have to reach police, they must. What happens?" Aarav says.

"It is compulsory to give a police complaint?" Riya asks with tension.

"Why are you tense? You did something wrong." The tension in Riya's voice makes Vibha doubt her.

"No, what did I do? I'm just scared." She looks really scared.

"Ok, I am Aarav, going to inform the head," Vibha went from there.

They are waiting for Vibha in her cabin. "Is he working at any gold-related company?" Aarav asks Riya.

"No, he is a civil engineer," Riya says. The sadness on her face makes Aarav not ask anything.

"Head told to inform the police," Vibha entered, and all of a sudden, she said.

"Really!!!" With wide-open eyes, suddenly he noted something on Vibha. He came near to her. She was speechless, staring at him with confusion. "What happened?" Aarav asks, holding her hand. It was a little wounded.

"Ooh, it is... When I was coming out of the room, a person came in front of me. I bumped into him, and I fell," Vibha says just like that. "He was so kind. You know he helped me to get up and said sorry also," Vibha says with a smile.

"Kind... ok," Aarav says while nodding his head.

"You can talk about this with Kavin. He can help us," Vibha gave an idea to him.

"Yes, I tried, but he was busy. I will talk to him later," Aarav says about the morning's incident.

"Ohh," Vibha added.

"Ok, come, we will inform the police." They went to the front bench.

Vibha's phone rings. She says, "What, sir, but why?" Vibha asks while looking at Aarav, shockingly. She hangs up the call and silently looks.

"What happened?" Aarav was looking scared.

"It's head," Vibha says with a sad face.

"What did he say?" Aarav asks with confusion.

"He said not to give a police complaint," Vibha says.

"Why?" Aarav became tense with this. They both stared at each other with confusion.

13

"What type of game have you created?" Nithin asks Neel.

"Come, I will show you." Neel wants to keep it a surprise.

They went to Neel's home; he was so excited to show the game to his friends. He took them to his gaming room. He has lots of gaming characters in his room. Finally, he shows his game to them.

"First, I will tell you about this game, ok. It is a historical game in which there was a king, queen, and soldier. Players can choose any character; the king and queen are both the best warriors, so both have the same powers. The opposite country will attack the king and queen; they must win the battle. If you win in the battle, it means the palace will be beautifully decorated in the past, but when you fail to save the kingdom, it means the king's palace will fall." Neel explained what the game was.

"Wow, Neel, you are so talented." Mithra appreciates Neel.

"He is talented, but a little stupid," Nithin says while tapping on Neel's shoulder.

"How did you get the idea to create this game?" Mithra asks with surprise.

"You had dreamed this right; you told me that dream," Nithin said with shock, his mouth open.

"Ohh! Nithin, you are my best friend. How could you remember this after these many days also?" Neel hugs him.

"Dream?" Mithra has no idea.

"Yes, he told me he frequently gets this dream," Nithin says.

"What? You never told me about this." Mithra was so wonderful about this.

"I think it was not that important while talking. One day I just told him, that's it," Neel tries to console her.

"Ok, tell me what happened," Mithra was so curious.

"I've been getting this dream for three years. It is not like a nightmare; whenever I get this dream, I feel sad and happy, and every emotion will come. It won't come every day when I went to the psychologist, but no use. So, I thought about making a game on that. I think I will get answers for my every question, but I didn't get any answer," Neel ends his flashback.

"Ok, leave definite one day you get," Mithra motivates him.

"Shall we play this?" Nithin was excited to play.

"Yes, you can. I feel something is missing in this game. I don't know what that was. That's why I brought you both. Can you help me?" Neel became sad.

"No, if you get me snacks, then only we help you," Nithin makes him normal.

"We! Really, you are an idiot." Neel became normal as Nithin thinks.

"Come, let's start the game."

They started playing a game. They are so happy enjoying their weekend. After playing the game, they are becoming so tired. They cooked lunch and had fun. Mithra was wondering while seeing Neel's collection in his house.

"Neel, you are so obsessed with historical things. Wow, these pots are so amazing, the art in them," Mithra was looking around the house, she liked his house filled with old collections.

"My mom used to collect these things from her. I got this interest," Neel became sad after talking about his mom.

"Don't worry, your parents will be seeing you from heaven. They feel proud of you," Mithra tries to console him.

"I never thought they could leave alone on the road. You know I can't forget that incident." Neel's eyes dropped to tears.

Neel's parents have died in an accident. Two years ago, his parents went on a trip. While coming back from the trip, they got in a bad accident. It was a hill station. Their car fell from the mountain. It made the police search for their body and got in bad condition.

"Hey guys, what are you doing? Come, we will watch a movie," Nithin calls them. He never wants Neel to be upset.

They started watching. Mithra got a call from Manasvi.

"Hi Manasvi, where are you? Is your work finished?" Mithra asks.

"My work has finished where you are?" Manasvi asks.

"We are in Neel's home watching a movie. Come join us," Mithra asks her to join them.

"Ok, I'm coming. My company is near to his, so I will be there in five minutes," Manasvi wants to join them. They ended the call.

"What does she say she is coming?" Nithin is curious.

"No, she is going for lunch with her team," Mithra lied to him.

"Lunch? Now she is eating lunch? Okay, say where they are going." Nithin questions.

"That Fosia Restaurant," Mithra says.

"Ohh," Nithin became moody. "Oh, my head is aching so much I can't watch a movie. I am going home." He wants to go from there.

"But you only ask us to watch a movie," Neel says.

"Ok, first please bring me cold water; after that, you go," Mithra says. He brought her water.

"Bye," Nithin says with a faint voice. He went Mithra and Neel were hidden, watching him.

After a minute, the doorbell rang. Neel went to open the door.

"Hi, Manasvi, come in," Neel welcomes her. "Hey, Nithin, you are still here. What happened? Did you forget something?" Neel asks Nithin, after seeing Manasvi, he comes back.

"What...Forgot," Manasvi said with confusion. "He says he came out to put out trash," Manasvi says.

"Trash... He went... Neel wants to say something, but Nithin closes his mouth. Manasvi smiled at Nithin and went inside.

They watch a movie together and have snacks.

"Ok, it's getting dark. We have to move," Mithra says after watching the movie, they are ready to go home.

"Shall I drop you guys off? It's already dark, and both of you are going," Nithin pointed to Mithra and Manasvi.

"Ok," Manasvi says. Nithin was happy to hear this, and they all went from there.

The sunset beautifully renders the throne to the moon.

14

"Do you think she can do this?" Kapil asks this in front of everyone.

"No, I know she never did this," Kavin says.

"How can you say this to her?" Kapil says with sad eyes on Kavin.

"Don't know. Still, I can't process this, but I have to do this. How much I love to work more. I love her so, I have to do this." Kavin looks confident.

"Then we call her tomorrow at 10:00 AM," Kapil says, looking at everyone.

"Where we are investigating her," Rahul asks, expecting an answer from Kavin.

"In the official investigating room itself," Smith says before Kavin opens his mouth.

"No problem, we'll call her there itself," Kavin accepted.

"Ok, inform her," Kapil says to Kavin.

"What? We can't do this if she was not that killer; it is okay, but if she is, that means she can erase every piece of evidence that is against her, so we can't know," Yuan says. Everyone is shocked, looking at him, but the point he makes is right, so one speaks.

"Ok, you all can believe me. I know she is not that type. If she is (stops), it means punishment is the same for everyone," Kavin says. The truth is, his eyes make everyone speechless.

"Then we can analyze all details once again," Smith says.

"Yes, first we have to check camera recordings," Kavin says, telling Kapil to play recordings.

They started to check the camera recorders of Sicilian from Yamni homes around the streets that are filled with cameras. The search for that red car. They are so careful. Their eyes are moving here and there, searching for the car to find where it went. So. They have checked so many records of the previous days. But they were like everything was normal. Nothing is suspicious. They are breaking their heads. They found nothing. The killer is so hard to mark. He was then. We were there, and there were no cameras.

"Kapil So, can I get them? Blueprint of Sicilian." Kavin asks Kapil.

"Yes, come in. I have a blueprint. Wait a minute; I will bring it. Kapil went to take the blueprint. He brought the blueprint to Kavin and gave it to him.

"With the cameras, all its data is in symbols. This is the camera blue printer here. We can know where the cameras are. Camera Blueprint. Weather camera for. It's marked with red for your point. Mention the camera.

"This is that long way where she went off, and there is no camera," Kavin says.

Everyone is carefully watching the blueprint. Marking following that, we were where they can go.

"Yes, see, from this street, they can go like this to Ishtan. Like that, the killer went." Sultan added.

They found how the killer went from Yamini St to Ishtan Pond. They are so surprised.

"He's so brilliant. He knows where the camera is, and where there is no camera, it means. He constantly goes to the street to note where the cameras are," Smith says while thinking.

"Then. He must be going there like a normal person," Rahul added.

"No. he thinks he does have. This blueprint," Sultan says, "because it is hard to go and note these things." He thinks in different ways. Everyone thinks from the Sultan's perspective.

"What do we have to do now?" Kapil asks.

"Go in his way. We can get it. Something that he missed," Kavin said with his red eyes and looking furious.

"Ok, we will go tomorrow," Rahul says while looking at Kavin.

"Search every corner. No one is perfect. He will leave something," Kapil says to Rahul.

"What about Yamini's mom? Is she OK?" Kavin asks Kapil.

"She was admitted to the hospital. They were unconscious on the street." Kapil gave information about Yamini's mom.

"Ohh," Kavin replied to him.

"Ok, I am exhausted. I will take some rest," Kapil says and goes to his room. There was a room where they could take a rest.

They are discussing Aksana and Shefali's deaths and checking recorders.

"Give me their forensic report," Kavin asks Rahul. He gave it to him. Kavin was checking reports again and again.

Kevin's phone rings. It was Mithra. He hesitated to attend the call. Everyone was looking at him. He came to the resting place. They ended again. She called; he was still thinking of attending. At last, gain confidence and attend.

"Kavin, what happened? Where are you? You did not call the day full. What happened? Did you eat? I know you're at work, but... I'm worrying about you. Tell me, what are you doing?" She builds a wall of questions.

"I'm at work. It's a big case." He gave a short answer to her wall of questions.

"Did you eat?" She understood with his voice that he was sad.

"No," he says woefully.

"What? Did you not have dinner? First, eat food, then work," she cares for him.

"You know how much I love my work, and it was my dream job," Kavin says, wanting to say something.

"Yes, I know what happened," she says, expecting him to talk.

"In this profession. I should not have any personal feelings. So, tell me if I have to investigate my relatives or friends. Whom I know very well. What do I have to do?" He doesn't know what to ask her.

"They are accused or not; it's secondary. But the first is. You have to be loyal to your profession. If you step out from it, it means the innocent will be punished. I don't know what you are talking about, but believe in yourself." She consoled him.

"Thank you, and sorry I was so confused; you made me feel better." Kavin's heart was filled with sadness and guilt for her.

"Everything will be alright." She makes him feel better.

"If I do something, be with me. Just believe me," he says with tears.

"OK, I will," she promised him.

"Love you. Take care," he said with love in his words.

"I love you so much, bye," she ended the call.

Kavin sadly leaned on the wall. There was someone in the bed. It was Kapil.

"I know what you are undergoing now, and I know she never does that," Kapil says with confidence.

"Thank you, Uncle," Kavin says with a smile.

"Take some rest. You are so confused." Kapil's concern for Kavin made him feel better.

"Ok," Kavin says in a low voice. He went to take a rest. Kapil and others are analyzing every detail. They became tired.

"I am hungry," Rahul says with a tired voice. "Me too," Smith follows him.

"Let's order something delicious," Rahul says with a joyful smile.

"We should not order here. It's a secret place," Yuan says with a firm face.

"What you all want to say, I will buy it for you all," Sultan says.

"Wow," Rahul and Smith said at the same time. Everyone says what they want. Sultan went out to buy food. Yuan also joined him.

"Yuan never smiles, every time having a stiff face," Rahul says to Smith. "Yes, I too note him," Smith added.

They were chatting about their personal lives; they became close. After some time, Yuan and Sultan came. They had their dinner, and after that, they closed everything. Everyone went to take a rest.

15

In the morning, Kapil came to the table; he saw Kavin come from outside.

"Where did you go?" Kapil asks him.

"I feel hungry, so I brought breakfast," Kavin says with a smile.

"Yesterday you slept with an empty stomach," Kapil says.

"Yesterday everyone had dinner without me," Kavin says mockingly angry.

"I don't want to disturb you," Kapil says, seeing his confident face.

"Uncle, come fast; I brought it for everyone, Kavin says. He calls Kapil Sir while working.

"You did not sleep well," Kapil asks Kavin whether he slept or not.

"I just wake up early," Kavin says. One by one, everyone came. They got freshened up and came to the table. They had breakfast.

Kavin took his phone to call Mithra.

Mithra attends the call. Kavin was quiet.

"Kavin, what happened?" Mithra asks.

"Mithra…" Kavin was not able to say.

"Why are you so silent? What happened?" she kept on asking him.

"Mithra. You have to come to the police station today. By 10:00 AM," At last, he told her.

"Why?" she asks with confusion.

"You are a suspect in one case we want to investigate," Kavin says, controlling his emotion.

"Ooh, that's me. OK, I believe you. I'm coming. "She says she remembers what he told her yesterday. Everyone is staring at him.

"She said she's coming," he says, looking at everyone.

"We have more time, so before investigating Mithra, we have to investigate her in her office, as Yamini and she were working at the same office, Lovely Cosmetic," Kavin says.

"Yes, it will be very useful for the case," Smith says. Everyone accepted that it was a good idea.

"We also have to inquire about Yamini's mom," Sultan says.

"She was in the hospital; we have to go there," Kapil says while looking at Kavin.

"One more place we have to go," Kavin says.

"Where?" Smith looks confused.

"Murder spot," Kavin says with a serious face.

"There, we will be able to find something," Rahul says, looking like he wants to go there.

"Then, okay, I will go there with Rah…" Kavin wants to say this before completing his sentence. Yuan says, "I too want to come with you." Kavin looks at him and says, "Ok." "Rahul and Smith go to Yamini's office." "Mr. Kapil and Sultan go to the hospital."

"Remember that we have to come soon before 10," Kapil says with a dutiful voice.

"Ok," Rahul says with a smile.

"After that, everyone directly came to the investigating room," Kavin says.

Everyone moved from there quickly to do their given work. They look so serious about this with the given time, they must investigate. They took their cars and went.

༺

Kavin and Yuan were going to the murder spot while Kavin was analyzing the forensic report of Yamini.

"Every murder he did, somewhere after they died, he publicly put the dead body, and after that only he put paints on them," Kavin says.

"Yes, that's why the police never got any knife from the murdered place," Yuan says.

"We should not search for the Knife," Kavin says with a smile.

"Then what do we have to search for," Yuan has no idea.

"Paint, we have to search for a paint box or tin like that," Kavin says, looking at Yuan.

They reach the murder spot; they look everywhere but get nothing.

They are searching around the pond and on the road as well.

"Nothing is here," Yuan says.

"Yeah, there is nothing." Kavin got nothing too.

"I think he has perfectly done this," Yuan says. They're searching everywhere.

"Let's go; it's getting late," Yuan says. They moved from there; after searching for an hour, they got nothing.

৪৩

Kapil and Sultan went to see Yamini's mom. They asked for Yamini's mom and came to know the ward. No, and went to see her. The doctor came out from the ward.

"Hello, Doctor," Kapil says with a smile.

"Hello, Mr. Kapil. How are you?" The doctor knows Kapil before himself.

"Fine," Kapil says.

"What happened?" Doctor asks.

"Doctor, How is she?" Kapil asks the doctor.

"She was in her last days; her condition was too bad," the doctor says of the condition of Yamini's mom.

"What?" Kapil was shocked.

"She has cancer on her brain, and now the clot is bleeding," the doctor says, what the problem was.

"We can talk with her?" Kapil asks with a sad face.

"No, she was unconscious," the doctor told her. She was not able to talk.

"Ok, Doctor, anything mean, call me," Kapil says.

"Is there any problem?" Doctor asks.

"Yes, did you watch the news about the murder on Sicilian?" Kapil asks.

"Yeah, I watch." The doctor knows about the murder.

"That girl's mother is only this patient," Kapil says. Who is she?".

"Ohh. Ok, sir, I will inform you when she comes to consciousness, the doctor says.

"Ok, doctor, thank you," Kapil says.

They went from the hospital. They went to the investigation place.

16

Smith and Rahul went to Mithra's office.

"What do you think about Kavin's girlfriend?" Smith asks about Mithra.

"Why, I have to think about her," Rahul says with a mocking smile. Smith gave a state to him.

"Ok, I don't know what to say after the investigation; only we can come to any conclusion before that; we can't say anything," Rahul says what he thinks is.

"Think if she was the killer means what will be Kavin's mind state," Smith says with shock.

"Ahhh, he can't live happily," Rahul can't imagine.

They reached the office and went inside. There were securities. They showed their ID proof and went inside. They meant two girls, and they inquired about them.

"Do you know Mithra and Yamini?" Rahul asks those girls.

"Yes, who are you?" They ask him.

"We are police," Rahul says with attitude.

"Ooh, good morning, sir." They gave respect, and they were just scared by the word police.

"Ok, tell me, is there any clash between Mithra and Yamini?" Rahul asks.

"Mithra insulted Yamini very much," they said with a sad face.

"Why?" Smith asks.

"Yamini mixed harmful chemicals in the sample product, so Mithra slapped Yamini," one girl said.

"What?" Smith and Rahul were shocked.

"Yes, sir, it was Mithra's dream project," they explain.

"About what?" Smith asks.

"It was a CB project. The face cream made with cherry blossoms can erase our scar marks and reduce acne. It will also give natural brightness," one girl explains.

"Why does Yamini want to destroy this project?" Smith asks with confusion. "Mithra scolded Yamini in front of everyone." They had a sad face.

"Ooh! Why?" Smith asks.

"Yes sir," they said, clearing his confusion, "Yamini's mom has cancer, so she won't come properly, and even if she does, she won't work properly."

"Mithra knows about Yamini's mom," Rahul asks her.

"We didn't know one week before itself Yamini came to know about her mom's health," one girl says.

"Then how do you guys know this?" Rahul asks her.

"One day Yamini was sharing this with Sunaina; I heard it," one girl says.

"Ok, Mithra, behave the same with everyone as she would behave with Yamini," Smith wants more information.

"No, sir, she was so kind to everyone; she behaved rudely only with Yamini and Sunaina," they told a suspicious thing. Smith and Rahul see each other face to face.

"But for the project, she will be rude to everyone," they say.

"Ooh," Smith was still in shock.

"Ok, what about Yamini's character?" Rahul asks.

"She has an attitude. We don't talk with her," they say with an angry face.

"Sunaina and Yamini, they both are thick friends," one girl says. "They always argue with everyone," she added.

"Sunaina has a boyfriend, but Yamini is single," another girl says.

"We heard that Mithra asked for Yamini to put her on the CB project." They gave more shock to Rahul and Smith.

"She asked both Sunaina and Yamini, but Sunaina was in another project, so she got only Yamini," they added.

"That's it we know, sir," they said like they know little.

"Ok, thank you for helping us." Rahul and Smith thanked them and went to inquire about others.

"Is it true that Mithra was the reason for firing Yamini from the job?" Rahul asks one lady.

"Yes, sir, that day Mithra slapped Yamini in front of everyone," the lady told the same. They investigate everyone and also watch the camera recorders. At last, they investigate the chairperson. After that, they went from there.

∞

Kavin and Yuan reached the investigation office at the same time as Kapil and Sultan, who also came.

"Kavin, do you have anything?" Kapil asks him about the clue.

"No," Kavin says with a sad face.

"Don't lose hope," Kapil makes him better.

"Did Yamini's mom say something?" Kavin says to Kapil.

"Still, she was unconscious, and she doesn't know about Yamini's death," Kapil explains her health condition.

They went inside and arranged everything for investigation. Smith and Rahul came. They look so tired.

"What happened?" Kapil asks them.

"We inquire about everyone and the same thing," Rahul says. "Yes, Mithra was kind with everyone but not with Yamini and Sunaina," Smith says.

"Mithra wants them to work under her on her project," Rahul says, "And the project name is Cherry Bloomsome." They make everyone shocked.

They explained everything to them. Who all they inquired and what all they said. They showed a recorder of Mithra slapping Yamini in front of everyone. This made Kavin shocked; he was just seeing it with unbelievable eyes. Kavin's phone rings.

It's Mithra; he attends the call.

"Kavin is here on the street," Mithra says. She came for an investigation.

"I am coming outside; wait," Kavin said to her and ended the call. "She came," Kavin says, looking at everyone.

Mithra was waiting outside. Kavin saw her and went to her.

"Take this." Mithra removed her ring, which was given by Kavin while proposing to her.

"Why? What are you doing?" Kavin asks with wide-open eyes.

"I am not here as your girlfriend is here as a suspect in a murder case," she says with a smile, and she is casual.

"What do you think?" Kavin wants to say something.

"After solving the case, give this to me, OK?" Mithra stops him and says what she thinks.

"But," Kavin still tries to speak. But he stops himself.

"Shall we go in?" Mithra asks with a smile.

Kavin took her inside the investigation room. Yuan stops Kavin to enter the room. Kavin looks at him confused.

"Please stay in the monitor room; from there you can watch," Yuan stopped Kavin from entering the investigating room.

"But why should I not come in?" Kevin got rage.

"We have to investigate the suspect as a suspect, but here she is your girlfriend," Yuan explains why he should not come in.

"Yes, Kavin he is right" Sultan accepts Yuan's point. Everyone thinks it's right.

"Ok," Kavin accepted and went to the monitor room.

17

Yuan, Smith, and Sultan went inside the investigation room. Kavin, Kapil, and Rahul stayed outside and watched from the monitor room. They have completed all arrangements and started the investigation.

"Mithra, sit down," Smith says to her.

"Thank you," Mithra says, looking confident.

"You are a cosmetologist," Sultan started the question kindly.

"Yes," Mithra says.

"From how many years you know Yamini and Sunaina," Sultan asks her.

"I know them from school," she says with a smile.

"You have some personal issues with her," Sultan asks her about their problem.

"No, sir." She looks confident.

"Then why behave so rudely to them?" Smith asks her about her behaviour.

"She wants to spoil my dream project," Mithra says with bitter rage.

"So, you killed her," Yuan says.

"What? Why do I have to kill her?" Mithra asked, scared.

"Because she added sulfates to sample products," Smith says.

"No, I didn't do that," Mithra says. The eyes are scared.

"Then tell who murdered her," Sultan asks her.

How do I know that? Mithra was confused; she didn't know what they were talking about.

"Ok, what about Aksana and Shefali's murder?" Sultan asks her.

"I don't know about that." She was confused.

"How do you know him?" They show her they have taken from Yamini's home.

"He was my friend's boyfriend," she has no idea. "Please call Kavin." She stands up from the chair and calls Kavin.

"SHUT UP, SIT DOWN," Yuan shouts at her. She was scared and sat quietly.

Kavin was watching these things from the monitor room. He became furious about Yuan's behaviour, and he tried to go inside the investigation room.

"Kavin, stop." Kapil stops him from going to the investigation room. He doesn't want him to go in.

"I have to go there." Kavin didn't want to listen to Kapil. He tries to go there and tries to explain to him that he wants to go there.

"No, you should not go." Kapil didn't let him go. He tries his best to stop him.

"Look how he scared her." Kavin loses his control; the way Yuan shouts at Mithra makes him out of control.

"It's his duty, Kavin," Kapil thinks Yuan did right as police. What has been done that's right?

"What duty to shout at her like that?" Kavin didn't understand what he was trying to explain.

"Yes, they are inquiring about her, but she is not cooperating," Kapil explains what has been done.

"After asking about him, she behaves like this," Rahul says. His eyes are looking at Kavin's.

"What do you mean?" Kavin asks with a low voice full of rage in his eyes.

"We have to wait," Rahul says.

"Yes, let them do their job," Kapil added.

Kavin became quiet and stared, observing Mithra's behaviour. He still believes she does not want her to suffer. Tears and rage filled his eyes. He was biting his nails and watching her.

Here, Yuan added more questions.

"He was the killer arrested three months ago. Now he had died, and now someone is making his aim of killing Yamini and Sunaina. Who is that? Yuan wonders if Mithra was also involved in this murder.

"HE WAS KILLER (with shock). Sir, I don't know," Mithra says.

"Then why did you warn them on engagement?" Yuan asks. He was raising his eyebrows.

"WHAT?" Mithra asks with confusion.

They show her a video recording of Sunaina's inquiry.

"Now tell me the truth," Yuan asks.

"It was…" Mithra stops thinking.

"What? Tell me why you did that," Yuan asks. She was still thinking. "Is it true that you threaten them?" he asks her. Everyone was looking at her.

"Yes," Mithra says, staring at the photo of Aksana and thinking something.

"Why did you?" Yuan asks.

"It does nothing with this case," Mithra says, now looking sad and guilty.

"Say what that was?" Yuan asks with curiosity. Everyone looks serious.

"It was Zoya," Mithra said with tearful eyes. She looks sad and furious.

18

On the first day of tenth grade, some students from other sections shifted to our class. I searched for Manasvi but didn't come. We were speared last year. In that she too came, she was Zoya; she was innocent and introvert.

"They shifted here from section B; from now on, they too are your classmate." The class teacher said it was the first day, so the teacher was so energetic. "Take your seats; students gave space to them," the teacher says.

Everyone gave their self-introduction. When it is the first day of school or college, self-introduction is the worst feeling ever; we are forced to talk in a second language.

"My name is Zoya, and…" She says in a low voice that's it; after that, she never speaks a word.

Everyone introduces themselves, and now it is seat arrangement time. They altered the place according to height; it was a sad moment. This arrangement can cause us to separate from our friends. But Manasvi, my best friend, was in another section, so I didn't have to worry about this seat arrangement. Unfortunately, Zoya was my bench partner. After that, books have been given, and break time has been given. During break time and lunch, I used to be with Manasvi.

"Hi Manasvi," I said to her with a beautiful smile.

"Hey! Hi! Manasvi was so energetic.

We both went to the canteen. I used to be with her. In class hours, Zoya and I were sitting together but never talked more than a few words. I was wondering how shy she was.

"Are you Manasvi's friend, Mithra, right?" She knows my name, but the thing she knows is that I am Manasvi's friend.

"Yes." I am quite surprised. Now it's my turn to ask something.

"What is your name?" I ask. She looks at me with shock. I understand. "Sorry, I forgot," I apologized.

"I'm Zoya," she says.

After that, I don't want to talk to you. Everyone has this feeling if we never know that person properly; also, we used to hate them like that. I don't want to have a conversation with her.

"From how many years have you both been friends, she asks.

"We are childhood friends." It irritates me.

"You have only one friend," she asks.

"Haan, what?" I was shocked.

"You have only one friend," she repeated her question.

"No, I have a lot of friends," I try to avoid her.

"How many friends?" She asks.

I pretended not to hear, but she was looking at my face. "I didn't count." Again, try to avoid it.

"Uncountable?" She was shocked.

"Yes," I say.

"I have no friends." She says with a sad face,

"Really," I just never mind.

"I don't like to talk with anyone. I don't know why I want to be friends with you," she says with a smile.

"Ohh!" I'm in quiet shock.

The classes ended, and lunchtime came. I try to run from there and pack my stuff.

"Shall we have lunch together?" she asks.

"Sorry, I used to eat with Manasvi," I say, and in the practice of avoiding her, I didn't arrange my things. I just ran from there.

Manasvi was waiting for me. We had lunch together and told each other everything that happened today.

"She wants to be friends with you," Manasvi says.

"Yes," I say with a low voice.

"Then be friends with her," she says.

"Don't know why I feel like...I don't like her," I told her.

"Then tell her what you feel," she says.

"Ok, leave. I don't want to talk about her." I just try to stop talking about her.

"Why?" she asks.

"Don't know," my sad voice made her stop talking about her.

"It is Kavin's final year," she says. We have a good time together after having lunch.

We went to the restroom before the bell rang. After using the restroom, I came out, and in the corridor, I was waiting for Manasvi to come out.

"Mithra," a different voice called me. I turned; it was Zoya, and I didn't know how to react.

"What are you doing?" She asks.

"I am waiting for..." I started to explain.

"Hey!" Manasvi came. We three are looking at each other in the face.

"This is Zoya," I say to Manasvi.

"Hi," she says to Zoya.

"This is Manasvi," I say. Zoya didn't even smile.

"We know each other's names," Manasvi says.

"How?" I ask.

"Before coming to your section, she was in mine," Manasvi replied.

The bell rang. Zoya calls me to come with her, and I refuse. After some minutes I went to the class. The class has started, and I was late to the class.

"Excuse me, ma'am." The teacher already was in my class. She was the type of person who could take a class on the first day.

"Come in," she says.

I came to my place. I saw my place was so clean and things were arranged in my bag.

"You did this?" I ask Zoya.

"Yes, you left your things outside, so I..." she started explaining to me.

"Who told you to touch my things?" I shouted in a loud voice, and the whole class looked at me.

"What happened?" The teacher asks.

"Nothing, ma'am," I say.

"Listen, class," she started taking class. I looked at Zoya; she was scared.

"I don't like it if anyone touches my things," I politely say.

"Sorry," she says.

That was the last time I talked with her. The days went like this, and she was quiet. She never talked with me. I don't feel anything.

19

One day, Kavin proposed to me that day Zoya was absent. The next day I and Kavin were coming to school together. Usually, classes have started.

"You and Kavin are in a relationship," Zoya asks me.

"Yes," I say happily.

"How?" she asks.

"What?" I was confused by the question 'How' and what it means.

"From when?" She asks another question.

"Why are you asking?" I ask.

"Today I saw you both coming together," she says.

"Ohh!" "We love each other one-sidedly, but yesterday only he proposed to me," I told her.

"I too have a crush on him," she says.

"What?" I was shocked.

"Yes, one day he helped me from that day I fell in love," she says with a smile.

"When?" I started asking questions.

"I'll never forget the day we met," she said, a faraway look in her eyes. "It was the first day of school at the entrance gate. My leg twisted and fell; I got injured in my hand. That time a boy helped me; it was Kavin. He only said that I was injured when I saw the blood; that's it. I opened my eyes in the nursing room."

I raised an eyebrow. "And that's when you fell in love with him?"

She nodded casually. "Yes."

I was curious. "Why did the sight of blood affect you so much?"

She replied matter-of-factly, "I have erythrophobia."

I asked, "What's erythrophobia?"

"It's a fear of seeing blood," she explained.

I was taken aback. "Oh, I see."

She smiled wistfully. "He was a nice guy." She said, "He has a girlfriend now."

My tone turned slightly angry. "So?"

She just smiles and says nothing. I left it just like that, but the words 'I fell in love with him' were disturbing my mind.

In the evening, all students are going home. I saw a bullying gang bully a girl. It was Zoya. They're putting blood on her. It was animal blood. I hear her scream and turn. I thought of helping her, but I couldn't, so I left her. I saw those eyes looking at me with expectation. I came from there. If I accepted it, my heart would not accept it. So, I went to help her. But what I saw was that Advik was helping her. He held her hands and took her from there; now also those eyes looked disgusted at me. I will never forget it, and that's it. We never talk again. Every time I saw her with Advik, I heard they both were in a relationship. He was a rich guy.

"She loves him because of his money. She can do anything for money," the rumours spread over the campus.

Management called her parents and gave her TC (Transfer Certificate); after that, she left the school.

"Management dismissed her." Everywhere this news was spread.

She packed her things, and she was going. Those eyes are still looking at me. I can't see her like this. I ran to her.

"Zoya, I came to help you," I say.

"I believe you," she says. I never expected this.

"Zoya," I mutter to her because I don't have words.

"If you could be my friend," she says with a sad smile.

"I am sorry." My eyes are filled with tears.

"You scared that I would snatch your boyfriend," she says.

"No, not like that." I lied; she was correct. I thought like that.

"Believe your love, Mithra." She smiled at me.

She has a big scar on her cheek many times. I thought to ask her about this, but I didn't ask her, "This scar," as I touched her cheek. She just smiled and nodded her head.

"Zoya, where are you going now?" I ask her.

"Lyziden," she says was far away from the Sisalian.

"But," I was speechless.

"Do you know about ZARA ORPHANAGE?"

"I'm sorry. I'm sorry," I ask her, apologizing.

"I left something for you on the desk. Take it," she says.

Her father brought the car she went to. Those who never looked at me now expect those eyes to look at me just for once. But... She left me in the Guilt. After that, I went to the classroom, and I saw. A cube and one letter for me. It was fallen to the ground. It is the unsolved cube that I have till now. The letter was.

Dear Mithra,

The friend everyone needs.
Don't know why I want to be friends with you; everyone has that one person whom they have to be with in every situation.
If you could be my friend, it never happens.

You are Unsolved Cube.

Do you know what the unsolved cube looks like? It looks confused because every colour has its meaning. It looked perfect when it was in the same colour.
Here I gave you an unsolved cube. Forget everything, and you should not have a pang of guilt.

Solved it.

Don't confuse your feelings; let it go its way.
Trust your feelings and have hope for love.

- Zoya

She left me with that unsolved cube. I will never forget that, and still, I have a pang of guilt. I never forgive myself until it is unsolved.

20

Many years went by like this, but the guilt never changed. I remain unsolved and cubed. It remains here, and now I have it with me every time. I want to see her happy, so I try to search for her. Three years ago I went to Lyziden, and I became later.

Once I was late.

I think I got apologized

Again I was late.

But now she is not there to punish or forgive.

I went to Lyziden in an attempt to find the Zara Orphanage. I learned the heartbreaking fact there: Zoya had committed suicide five months before. I also found out about Zoya's boyfriend, Mahit. He unexpectedly got in touch with me and sent me a location when I was looking for him.

The address took me to the bridge where Zoya had committed suicide. "Are you Mahit?" My voice trembled as I asked. "Yes," he said, pain streaming in his eyes.

I said, "Zoya's boyfriend," as I tried to take it all in. Mahit's face broke as he nodded. "What happened to her?" Gently, I inquired. Mahit's expression twisted in pain. "She was murdered!" he screamed, trembling.

My mind was spinning in shock. Shouting, "One girl can bear anything, but not that one thing," Mahit said. He tightened his hold on my neck and demanded, "What was it?" My mind was blank, even though I tried to think.

Mahit's eyes were burning with anger and sorrow. His body shook as he cried, "Think!" Suddenly, he fell to the ground, unable to contain his emotions. He screamed, "She was raped," his body trembling violently. It was as though someone had punched me in the gut. "What?" My head reeled in dread as I whispered.

I cried.

Am burst

I lost

I'm nothing

I guilt

I'm stupid.

I failed.

Unsolved

I was furious, my eyes burning. "Who?" I insisted. "Advik," Mahit spat out in a poisonous tone. "Advik?" I said it again, attempting to locate the name. It clicked then. Shouting, "Yes, he's the monster," Mahit said.

Tension permeated the air as we stood quiet for a while. At last, Mahit raised his voice. "He's getting engaged tomorrow." I tightened my jaw. "Where?" I mentally noted the address when Mahit gave it to me.

I went to the engagement the following day, my heart blazing with rage. Advik was so happy that he didn't notice the tempest that was building inside of me.

With a phoney smile on my face, I walked up to him. "Hi, Advik." Mahit was standing next to me, his eyes burning with rage. Advik's face shifted from happiness to surprise. "You? What are you doing?

Aksana shuddered at his side. "Who told you to come here?" With a tone full of cynicism, I turned to Aksana. "Why are you so scared?" Aksana's face was marked with anxiety as her eyes darted wildly. With a forceful voice, Shefali stepped in. "Hey, who are you?" I gave a charming smile.

"I'm Zoya's friend." The look on Shefali's face wavered. "Zoya? Who is that? In a whisper, Yamini said, "Zoya..." I arched an eyebrow.

"Wow, at least you remembered." Sunaina appeared perplexed. "Who's Zoya?" I spoke icily as I turned to face her.

"The girl you all bullied in school and spread rumors about." Shefali's face went white. "What?" I grinned. "I think you all remember now." With a growl, Aksana said, "Shut up and leave!" With a sardonic gleam in my eyes, I grinned.

"You reap what you sow." Anger flushed Advik's face. "Get lost!"

Mahit's eyes were burning when he seized Advik's shirt. "Mark my words, you'll face the consequences." The tension between us was evident as we exited the engagement.

Mahit looked at me. "Want to see Zoya's grave?" I experienced a twinge of remorse.

"No." Mahit's face was gentle as he gazed at me. When I said, "I don't have the strength," Mahit gave a nod. "Okay." I didn't see Mahit again after that.

21

In the inquiry room, Mithra broke down in tears. "I didn't see Mahit again after that. I promise that I did nothing.

Kavin came in with tears welling up in his eyes. He gave Mithra a firm hug. "I believe you."

They started talking about the matter when they had calmed down.

"Is it possible that the bully gang...?" Kavin fell silent.

Mithra gave a nod. "It was Yamini, Aksana, Shefali, and Sunaina."

Smith's forehead wrinkled. "But who's behind the murders after Mahit?"

Kavin looked over at Mithra. "Did Mahit mention anything about revenge?"

Mithra gave a headshake. "No, he didn't say anything like that."

Sultan raised his voice. "What's our next move?"

Kavin had a determined look on his face. We must travel to Lyziden. We'll discover hints there."

౮

Rahul gave a nod of consent. "But it won't be easy, especially during election time."

There was worry in Kapil's voice. "We'll have to be careful."

Deep in contemplation, the group became silent. Thinking of Zoya's memory caused Mithra's eyes to water.

Sultan urged, "Sir, we need to get to Lyziden as soon as possible. We might find some clues."

Rahul nodded. "All the answers are waiting for us in Lyziden."

Kavin thought aloud, "They used blood on Zoya, so the killer used paint on the victims."

Yuan's eyes widened. "I think there's more to it. There wasn't just one killer—it was a team."

The group turned to Yuan, surprised by his revelation.

Rahul acknowledged, "You're right, Yuan."

Kavin asked Mithra, "What happened to Zoya's parents?"

Mithra's voice trembled. "They died in an accident."

Rahul wondered, "Why did Sunaina lie?"

Yuan observed, "People rarely admit their faults. They try to alter the truth to suit their situation." He glanced at Mithra.

Smith summarized, "So, we know now that all this is connected to Zoya."

Sultan added, "Someone is taking revenge for her."

Rahul's eyes widened. "But what about Advik? He was the main culprit behind Zoya's death."

Mithra's eyes flashed with anger. "Yes, he was."

Smith was perplexed. "But didn't he commit suicide?"

Rahul countered, "Why are we so sure it was a suicide?"

Yuan asked Mithra, "Why did you threaten them at the engagement?"

Mithra explained, "Mahit told me to do it. I thought he was planning to file a complaint."

Kavin pressed for more information. "What exactly did Mahit say?"

Mithra furrowed her brow. "He didn't say anything specific."

Yuan suggested, "It's possible that Advik's death wasn't a suicide."

Kavin concluded, "We need to head back to our place and regroup."

Kavin and Mithra stood alone outside as the others departed. Kavin's eyes were filled with sadness as he gazed at Mithra.

"Mithra," Kavin said softly, approaching her.

"I'm leaving," Mithra replied, her voice barely above a whisper.

"Mithra, did you leave Zoya when she needed your help because of me?" Kavin asked, his voice laced with guilt.

Mithra's smile was tinged with sadness. "I think so."

Kavin's eyes dropped. "I'm sorry."

Mithra's expression was confusing. "Why are you apologizing?"

Kavin's voice cracked. "I think I need to apologize for everything." He was sad; he thinks because of him, Mithra was facing these many things.

Mithra's eyes welled up with tears. "You don't need to apologize, Kavin. I'm the one who did something terrible."

Kavin tried to console her. "This wasn't your fault, Mithra. It was Advik's doing."

But Mithra was consumed by guilt. "If only I had been a better friend to Zoya, she'd still be alive. I killed her, Kavin."

Kavin wrapped his arms around Mithra, trying to calm her down. "No, Mithra, you didn't kill her."

After a while, Mithra composed herself, and Kavin drove her home. They sat in silence, the tension between them palpable.

As they reached her home, Kavin asked, "Did you eat something?"

Mithra nodded silently.

Kavin waited until she got out of the car and went inside before driving away.

Meanwhile, the others gathered at their secret meeting spot, discussing the Advik case.

Kavin joined them, and Kapil briefed him on their discussion.

Rahul explained, "We can't access the case files since it happened in Lyziden."

Kapil assured them, "I'll try to get permission to access the files."

Sultan pointed out, "The case will be handled in Lyziden."

Smith asked Rahul, "What do you think about the Advik case?"

Rahul replied, "I think it was murder."

Smith countered, "We can't jump to conclusions without evidence."

Yuan intervened, "But think about it—Advik raped Zoya and was living his life happily. Then Mahit threatened them, and suddenly Advik committed suicide. Doesn't that seem suspicious?"

Smith's eyes widened. "What are you saying?"

Yuan's voice was firm. "Advik was murdered."

The group fell silent, stunned by Yuan's revelation.

22

The group was enjoying their lunch together when Rahul's phone rang. He answered, "Doctor?"

Rahul's expression changed from calm to concerned. "What? What happened, doctor? Where? Now? Okay, I'll inform them."

Rahul ended the call, and the group's attention turned to him.

"What happened?" Smith asked, worry etched on his face.

Rahul hesitated before speaking. "It's Sunaina. Her condition has worsened, and they need to perform surgery."

Kavin's eyes widened. "Is it critical?"

Rahul's voice was laced with concern. "The hospital doesn't have an experienced doctor to perform the surgery, so they're transferring her to Wioora Hospital."

Kavin's brow furrowed. "Wioora? But that's far from here."

Smith nodded in agreement. "Yes, it's quite a distance."

Yuan explained, "Wioora Hospital uses advanced technology. It's probably the best option for Sunaina's treatment."

Rahul checked his watch. "They are transferring her now. We need to go."

Smith stood up. "Then let's go now!"

Kavin and Yuan nodded in unison. "Yes, let's go."

Kapil took charge. "Okay, come on, let's go to Wioora Hospital."

Rahul nodded. "Okay."

As they arrived at Wioora Hospital, Sunaina was being wheeled into the ICU. The doctors rushed to attend to her, taking scans and X-rays.

One of the doctors emerged from the ICU, and Kavin approached him. "Doctor, what's Sunaina's condition?"

The doctor hesitated. "Our head doctor will assess her and provide an update. He's the only one who can give you a clear picture."

The head doctor arrived, and the group greeted him. He exchanged medical terms with the other doctors before entering the ICU to examine Sunaina.

Kavin approached him again. "Doctor, what's Sunaina's condition?"

The head doctor looked at him. "You're Detective Kavin, I presume?"

Kavin nodded. "Yes, Doctor."

The head doctor explained, "The blood clot in her brain can be treated. Don't worry; she'll recover after her treatment. It's a mild case."

Kavin asked, "When will the operation take place?"

The doctor replied, "We'll administer TPA, a treatment for blood clots. It's a standard procedure."

Kavin pressed for more information. "When will the treatment start?"

The doctor casually replied, "Tomorrow."

Kavin's eyes widened in shock. "Tomorrow? But..."

The doctor reassured him, "Don't worry; it's a mild case."

Kavin nodded, still concerned. "Okay."

As the head doctor walked away, Kapil turned to Kavin. "What did he say? I didn't understand his behaviour."

Smith asked, "What's our next step, Kavin?"

Kavin pulled out his phone. "I'll reach out to my friend, Aarav, for help."

Kavin called Aarav, "Aarav, where are you?"

Kavin said, "No, I'll come to you."

Kavin ended the call and informed the others, "He's not able to come here."

Smith asked, "Who is he?"

Kavin explained, "Aarav is my friend, a general surgeon. I think he can help us."

Rahul asked, "Is he not coming here?"

Kavin replied, "He just came out of the operating theatre and is tired."

Kapil suggested, "We'll go to him. Sunaina is under observation, so there's nothing we can do here."

Kavin agreed, "Okay, let's go."

They headed to Aarav's cabin. Kavin entered, finding Aarav sitting on the sofa shirtless and sweaty.

Aarav asked, "Kavin, what's going on?"

Kavin apologized. "Sorry to disturb you."

The others entered, and Aarav greeted them. Rahul whispered to Smith, "Check out his abs."

Smith quieted him. "Shut up."

Aarav stood up, greeting Kapil, "Hello, Uncle."

Kapil smiled, "Hello, Aarav. How are you?"

Aarav replied, "I'm fine, Uncle. Thanks for asking."

Kavin explained the situation. "Aarav, I'm handling a serial killer case. One of the victims has a blood clot in her brain and is admitted here. The doctor said they will treat her tomorrow, but I need your help."

Aarav clarified, "I am a general surgeon, Kavin. I'm not sure I can help with neurology."

Kavin asked, "Is there anything we can do?"

Aarav offered, "I can ask my head to help. Maybe he can arrange something."

Aarav called his head, and after a brief conversation, he said, "My head will arrange for the treatment to start tonight."

Kavin and the others were relieved and thanked Aarav.

Aarav smiled. "Don't thank me yet. I need a favour from you guys."

Kavin's curiosity was piqued. "What is it?"

Aarav's expression turned serious. "I need your help with something."

23

Aarav said, "First, I'll call Vibha."

Kapil asked, "Vibha?"

Kavin raised an eyebrow. "Who's Vibha?"

Aarav reminded him, "She's my friend, Vibha."

Kavin chuckled. "Oh, I remember."

Aarav contacted Vibha, asking her to bring Harsha's report to his cabin.
Shortly after, Vibha entered the cabin.

"Aarav!" Vibha exclaimed, startled by the presence of so many people.

Aarav introduced her, "Everyone, this is Vibha, my friend and a cardiologist."

Vibha greeted the group, "Hello!"

Kavin replied, "Hello!"

Vibha's eyes widened in surprise, and she stared at Aarav, who was still shirtless.

Aarav quickly put on his shirt, and Vibha composed herself, trying to appear calm and professional.

Rahul whispered to Smith, "Should we arrest Aarav?"

Smith asked, confused, "Why?

Rahul whispered back, "He's seducing a woman."

Smith quieted him. "Shut up."

Aarav asked Vibha, "Please explain Harsha's case to Kavin."

Vibha shifted into professional mode. "Okay.

Aarav offered her a chair. "Please, take a seat."

Vibha began, "We found something suspicious about a patient who died. When he was admitted, he was already dead. The confusion is that we think it might be a murder."

Kavin's eyes widened in shock. "What?"

Aarav reminded him, "The boy from the cafe."

Kavin's expression changed to one of alarm. "He died?"

Kavin asked, "What happened?"

Vibha explained, "We thought it was a heart attack, but..."

Yuan pressed for more information. "But what?"

Vibha shared every detail she had previously discussed with Aarav. The group listened intently, shocked by the revelation.

Rahul's voice was laced with stress. "Suicide or murder... again?"

Smith quieted him with a gentle "Shh."

Rahul asked Vibha, "Why did your head refuse to file a complaint?"

Vibha replied, "I don't know. I asked him, but he didn't give me a clear answer."

Kavin suggested, "Aarav, can you ask your head for help?"

Aarav shared, "I already did." He told me not to get involved and to drop it."

Smith wondered, "Why is everyone refusing to help?"

Kavin's expression turned serious. "They're not refusing; they're scared of the truth."

Vibha asked, "What do you mean?"

Kavin explained, "Someone is silencing them."

Vibha questioned, "How can you be so sure?"

Kavin pointed out, "When you asked your head, he gave you permission, but then someone must have intervened."

Aarav's eyes narrowed. "So, what does that mean?"

Kavin's eyes locked onto Aarav's. "It means someone is involved, and we need to find out who."

Yuan suggested, "Think back to when you were talking to your head. Was anyone else around?"

Vibha thought for a moment. "No, we were alone. There was no one else."

Kavin started to speak, but Vibha interrupted him.

Vibha remembered, "Wait, when I came out of the cabin, someone bumped into me. I remember his face."

Kavin's eyes sparkled with interest. "Do you remember what he looked like?"

Vibha described, "He was handsome."

Rahul's eyes widened in shock, and the group turned to him.

Smith asked, "Why do you look so shocked?"

Rahul quickly covered, "Nothing."

Vibha glanced at Rahul, and he avoided eye contact. Smith raised an eyebrow, intrigued by Rahul's reaction.

Vibha clarified, "I mean, I've seen his face before."

Yuan suggested, "Should we get a camera recording?"

Aarav stood up. "I'll bring one."

Sultan offered, "Shall I come with you?"

Aarav declined, "It's okay."

But Sultan insisted, "No problem, I'll come."

Aarav and Sultan left the room.

Yuan asked Vibha, "What's Harsha's girlfriend's name?"

Vibha replied, "Riya."

Yuan wondered, "Do you think she could be capable of murder?"

Vibha shook her head. "No, she looks weak."

Smith whispered to Rahul, "Why is Yuan asking about Riya?"

Rahul whispered back with a sly smile, "He's single, and now she's single too."

Yuan's voice turned cold. "What's going on?"

Rahul and Smith chimed in unison, "Nothing."

Aarav and Sultan returned, looking confused.

Kavin asked, "What happened?"

Sultan explained, "There's no footage from that time. All the recordings from that particular time have been deleted."

Rahul's eyes widened in shock. "What?"

Kapil asked, "Only from that specific time?"

Aarav confirmed, "Yes."

Kavin's expression turned serious. "Something's suspicious."

Yuan agreed, "It's murder."

Sultan nodded in agreement. "Yes."

Kapil reassured Aarav, "Don't worry; I'll inform the police to investigate this further."

Kavin explained, "We're already working on a big case, and we need to go to Lyziden for investigation."

Aarav understood, "Oh, okay."

Kavin apologized, "I'm sorry."

Aarav waved it off. "No need to apologize. What can you do when you're not able to?"

Kapil promised, "I'll inform my higher officials."

Aarav thanked him. "Thank you, Uncle."

Kapil smiled. "It's our duty."

Sultan asked, "Can we leave now?"

Rahul's eyes sparkled with surprise. "Why?"

Smith teased him, "What, you want to stay here?"

Rahul played along, "Yes."

Smith was confused. "What?"

Rahul clarified, "I mean, Sunaina's treatment is starting tonight."

Smith understood, "Oh."

Kavin said, "You can stay here. We're leaving."

Rahul's face lit up. "Really?"

Kavin smiled. "Yes."

Smith offered, "I'll stay with him."

Kavin agreed, "Okay."

The others bid farewell and left.

Kavin said, "Okay, bye, and thank you."

Aarav waved goodbye. "Bye."

24

Kavin and his team are in their place. Rahul and Smith looked tired.

"What happened?" Kavin asks.

"I am exhausted," Rahul sat on a chair.

"You did the surgery," Kapil teased them.

"We didn't sleep," Smith says with a tired voice.

"I want to sleep," Rahul murmured.

"Go take a rest," Kapil says to them.

"Thank you, Mr. Kapil," Smith says while going. "Good night, everyone," Rahul says.

"What good night? It's morning," Kapil asks.

"Bye," Rahul went. Kapil was smiling in cuteness.

Kavin phones ring at Manasvi.

"Hello," Kavin says.

"HOW DARE YOU, you investigate Mithra, an accused? I didn't expect this from you," Manasvi shouted at him. "No Manasvi," he tries to explain.

"I never expect?" She was not listening to his words.

"First listen to my words," he asks.

"What you want to say," she asks furiously.

"The Sicilian serial killer..." He explains what happened.

"So, to prove them you did this to my friend," she thinks, what Kavin did was wrong.

"I'm sorry I'm in that situation," Kavin says sadly.

"I don't want to talk with you," she was out of switch.

"Manasvi lies..." Kavin tried, but she ended the call. He was sad and thinking about that.

৳৹

Time moves Kapil came to the table. There was no Kevin, but everyone was there.

"We are going to Lyziden," Kapil says happily.

"Really?" Rahul was surprised.

"Yes," Kapil confirms.

"When?" Yuan asks

"After two days," Kavin replied.

"Ooh, okay," Yuan's expression.

"Ok, where is Kavin?" Kapil asks them.

"He was taking a rest," Smith says. Kapil went to see Kavin.

He was sitting on bread sadly.

"What happened?" Kapil asks him.

"Nothing, Uncle." He doesn't say anything about Manasvi's call.

"Are you ok?" Kapil asks him with care.

"I'm okay. What happened?" he asks. Kapil says about going to Lyziden after two days.

"There are two days," Kavin says.

"Yes," Kapil says.

"Ok, Uncle, I am going home; I have unfinished work," Kavin says.

"Ok," Kapil says.

Everyone went to their home for two days. Kavin met Neel, Nithin, and Manasvi.

He explains everything to them. He found that the killer was Zoya's boyfriend. Mithra and Zoya's incident; now they are going to Lyziden.

"It's ok; I understand." Manasvi finally understands Kavin.

"Are you going Lyziden?" Neel asks.

"Yes," Kavin says.

"Ok, all the best," Neel says.

"Don't reveal this," Kavin says to keep it a secret.

"That's hard," Neel says while seeing Manasvi.

"Be quiet." Nothing controlling Neel.

"Shut up; don't worry. I won't tell anyone," Manasvi says.

൭

Two days later, the team gathered at their place. They were ready to go to Lyziden; they packed everything and went from Sicilian. It was a long journey.

"We will reach Lyziden at night," Kapil says.

"What?" Rahul was shocked.

"In travel itself, one day will move," Smith says.

"Yes," Kapil confirmed.

"Don't worry, directly we will go to the hotel; the next day morning we start working," Kavin says with a smile.

"Ok," Rahul said with a little satisfied face.

"First, we will investigate Advik's case," Kavin says.

"Yes," Kapil accepted.

"Yes, after that we will go to Zara Orphanage," Kavin says what they have to do.

"We have to investigate Zoya's case," Kapil says.

"Yes, there is much work," Sultan replies.

"Please don't scare me," Rahul says with a sad smile.

"Shut up." Smith did his job.

"What happens in a hospital?" Kavin asks about Sunaina's surgery.

"Vibha works in the morning, so she was not there," Rahul is talking about Vibha.

"But I ask about Sunaina," Kavin says with confusion. Everyone was laughing at Rahul.

"She is ok," Smith says. And told me about the treatment.

"I'm sleepy. Good night," Rahul says to avoid the awkward situation.

"Good night, but it's morning," Kavin says with a smile.

25

In the morning, the sun rises beautifully, and someone knocks on Kavin's room door. Kavin opens his room door; it's Yuan.

"What happened?" Kavin asks him.

"It's time to work; are you still sleeping?" Yuan asks.

"No, I went to the bathroom," Kavin says.

"Ok, come fast," Yuan says.

&

All went to the Lyziden police station. They give details of Advik's case, and the policeman, Mr. Lee, was helping them.

"Why the orange paint put on him?" Kavin asks with shock.

"He fell from a fifty-floor building. The building construction was not done when he fell; there was a painting in which one paint fell on him," Lee explained.

"It was not an accident," Kavin says.

"What?" Lee was shocked. Kavin explains everything to him. He was stunned.

"Till today I thought it was suicide." Lee was shocked and couldn't process it.

"Can I see his postmortem report?" Kavin asks him.

"No, we didn't do a postmortem," Lee says.

"What?" Kavin was shocked.

"But it was a suicide now," Yuan asks him.

"Yes, his father was a rich person. He used influence. He didn't allow us to do a postmortem," Lee clarified.

"Then how do you finalize that he committed suicide?" Yuan asks him.

"When we investigated Advik's fiancé, she told us that after the engagement, he was wrong; like, he says that he doesn't want to get married after that he died," Lee says.

"You did not search in his home?" Kavin asks.

"No, his dad doesn't want it to spread, so he tries to close this case soon," Lee says.

"It's disbelieving," Rahul was shocked.

"We have a search on his home; then only we can get any information," Kavin says.

"I have to ask permission," Lee says and goes from there.

"Ok," Kavin says. They are discussing this.

"I think his father knows that Advik has raped Zoya, so that's why he is urgent to close this," Rahul says.

"Haan, his father doesn't want to spoil his name," Smith says.

"You are right," Kavin thinks it was the reason.

Lee came "We have a search warrant. We go now," he says.

"Wow, let's go now." Rahul was excited.

They went to Advik's home and showed the warrant to his parents.

"What is this?" Advik's father asks with anger.

"We reopened the Advik case," Lee says.

"WHO GAVE PERMISSION?" Advik's father shouts.

"Please move aside; let us do our work," Kavin says and moves him aside.

"Where is his room?" Lee asks

"First floor, left side," one maid says.

They went to his room and searched. They didn't leave any corner.

"SIR!" The sultan shouts in shock.

"What happened?" Everyone was shocked.

"Cube with a letter," Sultan says.

"Cube?" Lee asks.

"Letter?" Rahul asks at the same time.

"Look," Sultan shows the letter and cube.

Rahul took the letter and read it; he was shocked.

"What happened?" Smith, snatch the letter from Rahul.

"Sunaina will die soon.

-Zoya" Smith read it aloud. Everyone was shocked.

"Zoya?" Yuan asks.

"She was dead," Kavin says with confusion. All read that letter and were surprised.

"Someone was trying to stop us," Yuan says.

"Ask Advik's father if anyone came here," Kavin says.

They asked Advik if anybody had come here before they were coming.

"Yesterday there was a prayer meeting," Advik's father says.

"Prayer meets?" Kavin asks him.

"My wife has died," Advik's father says.

"Who all came?" Kavin asks.

"My company partners, staff, and cleaners all came," Advik's father replied.

"We want to check camera footage," Kavin asks.

"Took them," Advik's father told the maid.

"Who all is working here?" Kavin asks.

"Me, cleaner lady, gardener, and watchman," she says.

"Ohh! You all stay here," Kavin asks.

"No, sir," she says.

"Who stays here?" Kavin asks.

"Nightwatchman will stay here." She looks normal.

"From how many months have you been working here," Kavin was adding a question.

They saw recordings, but there was no recording on a particular day.

"Someone has erased it," Kavin says.

"No, at that time all the cameras are off," Sultan says he was checking.

"What?" Yuan was shocked.

"Sunaina was in danger. We have to do something," Smith says.

"Yes, sir, tell them to give police protection," Kavin told Kapil.

"Ok," Kapil went to inform.

"What killer is not going to kill on November 6?" Rahul says.

26

"Why was the letter kept with Cube?" Smith asks with confusion.

"Mithra says Zoya gave the cube to her. What if... Rahul says stop; realizes Kavin is there.

"What if? Complete the sentence," Yuan asks.

"What if Mithra kept that cube?" Rahul, complete the sentence.

"I don't think I met her yesterday. Also, how can she come and keep this? Kavin says he believes in her.

"Why does she have to come? She can get help from someone else," Yuan says.

"But she says everything, and she doesn't meet Mahit," Sultan supports Kavin.

"What if she lied?" Yuan says.

"There is not only one cube; there are many. It is like someone wants to frame her," Sultan says.

"I know her well; she can't do that," Kapil says he came after informing the police to give protection to Sunaina.

"Sorry, Kavin, she is your girlfriend, but for us, she is a suspect," Yuan strongly thinks Mithra was a killer.

"If she does also, what is the motive?" Kapil asks.

"Guilt" yuan simply connects everything.

"What? Kapil was shocked.

"Yes, she only told him she felt guilty," Yuan explained.

"Please, Yuan," Kapil asks him to shut up.

"Please, Mr. Kapil, that's why this case went long," Yuan says he doesn't want to be quiet.

"What do you want to say?" Kapil asks.

"If you listen to Yamini and Sunaina's words, it means it won't happen what is happening now," Yuan was frustrated with these guys.

"Please, we are not in court to argue; we are in the victim's home," Smith tries to control.

"You do not have strong evidence; let's go now," Kapil says.

"Yes, we should not say it just like that," Yuan was thinking.

They went from there and went to their place.

Next, everyone is sitting in a group discussion in Kavin's room.

"What happened? You found something?" Kapil asks Kavin.

"My mind was blank," Kavin says.

"Sorry, without evidence. I say those things. I was frustrated because she is your girlfriend. If you save her, that's why," Yuan asks for apologies.

"Sorry, I gave you space to think about this. Punishment is for everyone who did wrong. I won't save any accused. If she did, that means I will arrest and give punishment, I promise," Kavin's promise.

"We have to go to Zara orphanage," Kavin says.

"Before that, I want to say one thing," Rahul says.

"What?" Kavin asks.

"The cube..." Rahul wants to say something.

"AGAIN," Smith says. "Let him finish," Rahul says with scared eyes.

"When Mithra says about Zoya's cube and in the letter also written Zoya with the cube," Rahul says.

"So," Yuan asks.

"I think Zoya likes Cube so much that he is killing them using different paints on victims, like how they pour blood on Zoya, and he tears their cheek as Zoya's cheek."

"Yes, but he pours paints on them not for cube; I can't understand what you are saying," Smith was so confused.

"Oh god, he uses colour, which is in the cube," Rahul says.

"What?" Smith did not understand.

"What are all the colours he uses?" Rahul asks.

"He uses green, yellow, and white," Yuan says.

"No use orange also," Sultan reminds.

"What?" Rahul asks with confused eyes.

"Ohh, yes, on Advik," Smith remembered.

"Yes, now check what colours the cube has," Rahul says.

"Green, Orange, White, Yellow, Blue, and Red," Smith says, seeing that cube that they got yesterday at Advik's home with the letter.

"What colours are remaining?" Rahul asks.

"Wait, green, red... Haan, Blue and Red," Smith says, confused.

"Next, he was going to use two colours," Rahul says with a proud face.

"He was going to do two murders?" Smith asks.

"How?" Yuan was shocked.

"How? There is only one victim. It's Sunaina," Rahul became sad.

"Two murders?" Sultan repeated it.

"You are right; you found the meaning of cube," Kavin says.

"But who is the last one?" Sultan says.

"I think I found it wrong." Rahul was confused and sad.

"No, why does it have to be the last one if he kills that person before itself means," Kavin says.

"What could be the reason?" Rahul asks.

"For that, we have to know about Zoya's life," Yuan says.

"Zoya's life?" Rahul asks.

"Yes," Yuan says.

"Who will tell?" Rahul asks. He has many doubts.

"We have to go to that orphanage," Yuan says, where they can get.

"I think we have to discuss this with Mithra," Rahul says.

"MITHRA!" Smith was shocked.

"Why?" Kavin asks.

"I think it will be helpful if we ask her about that letter," Rahul says.

"Yes, she has Zoya's written letter," Yuan says.

"But we talk in video calls only," Rahul says.

"Yes," Yuan agrees.

"Ok, I will inform her." Kavin accepts that idea.

27

Kavin contacts Mithra to talk about this. Rings goes she didn't attend the call; after some time, she attended the call.

"Kavin, what happened?" Mithra was scared because he called her many times.

"Mithra, what happened?" Kavin asks at the same time.

"I was taking a bath; that's why I was not able to attend the call," Mithra says.

"Ok," Kavin relaxed.

"What happened?"

"That's what we want to talk about: Zoya's letter that you have because here we got a letter written by Zoya," Kavin explained to her.

"What was written by Zoya?" Mithra was unbelievable.

"Yes," Kavin says.

"But she died three years ago," she says.

"Yes, that's why we want to check the handwriting, so you keep that letter ready," Kavin says.

"Ok, but I will call you after some time," she says.

"Ok." Kavin ended the call and informed everyone, "She will call later."

"Ok," Kapil nodded.

"Shall we have breakfast? Please, I am starving," Rahul said, holding his stomach and baby face.

"Ok, let's order something," Kavin says, and they have ordered food. They were having their breakfast when Lee entered.

"Lee, come join us," Kapil says with a smile.

"Today we can't go to the orphanage," Lee says with a sad face.

"WHY?" Rahul was shocked.

"They went for a trip. Tomorrow morning, they will come, so we go by evening," Lee explains.

"What is this... what we will do now?" Rahul was sad and exhausted with this case.

Mithra called Kavin, and he attended. "Mithra, are you ready? Can I do a video call?" Kavin asks her whether she is ready. They arranged everything and made a video call for Mithra.

"Hi Mithra, do you know about Advik?" Kavin asks her with a worried face. He doesn't want her to be in this case.

"Advik...Yeah, I heard that he committed suicide," she says, what she heard from others.

"It was murder," Kavin reveals the truth.

"WHAT?" She was never expecting this answer.

"Yesterday we went to his home for a search. That time we got..." Kavin wants to explain.

"What you got?" she was curious.

"The Letter and Cube," he says with hesitation.

"CUBE?" She was out of the water.

"Yes," he politely says.

"Is it solved?" She wants more information about the cube.

"It looks like half solved." He has no idea why he is asking.

"Show me." She wants to see the cube.

"Here, look." He showed the cube to her.

"It's not half solved; less than half of it has more to solve." She says her eyes are stocked in a cube, and it's filled with tears.

"Ohh" He doesn't know that much about the cube.

"You said you got a letter too," she was asking about the letter.

"Yes, we want to ask about that, but still you have Zoya's letter with you," Kavin came to the point.

"I have" She was confused.

"Show," he ordered her.

"What happened?" She has no idea.

"The letter we got from Advik House is written by Zoya," he says, his eyes carefully watching her.

"WHAT ZOYA?" She was shocked and looked unbelievable.

"Look, it has been mentioned here." He showed her the name of a writer on the corner.

"It's Zoya; it's Zoya's handwriting." She was scared by the fearful tears. The eyes are rolling with disbelief.

"WHAT? Are you sure?" He asks her with wide-open eyes.

"Yes, I can't forget that handwriting," she seems sure.

"But you only told me that she committed suicide," he asks her.

"They told me like that only," she says while thinking of when she visited the orphanage.

"Who?" He speaks.

"Mahit and the lady in the orphanage," she says. Her eyes are recalling the day. "Mahit asks me to visit Zoya's grave, but I refuse." She was confused by this letter.

"Why do you refuse?" He says he has no idea; some silence took place. Everyone was looking at her.

"The word 'If you could be my friend' makes me refuse," she says the guilt kills her more.

"So, you did not go to her grave?" Kavin wants to make sure. She nodded her head yes.

"Kavin, what? Zoya is alive?" She asks with little hope.

"We don't know. Tomorrow we are going to the Orphan, and after that, we will check Zoya's room," he says his plan to her.

"Zoya's room." She was worried.

"Yes, we found that the killer was going to murder two more people. The one we know was Sunaina, but the last person doesn't know who that was. He speaks.

"I want to come with you." She was stunned and thinking of Zoya and wanted to join him.

"But it..." he tries to refuse her because it was a secret operation.

"Please, I will be helpful, please." She was desperately wanting to come.

"Ok," Yuan says, looking at Kavin. He permitted her.

"Careful," Kavin says with concern. They understand her feelings.

"Bye," Mithra ended the call.

"I think we have to reopen Zoya's case," Yuan says. He looks sure about this.

"What?" Kapil was shocked.

"Do you think she is alive?" Kavin asks him. Yuan nodded his head, but he was not sure.

"Lee, get information about Zoya's case," Kavin says. It seems he is confused about Zoya's case.

"It was a little hard for Chief Police to handle it." Lee says, "I will try," after thinking he says he will try.

28

The next morning, Kavin waited at the railway station, his eyes scanning the crowd for Mithra. When she arrived, a soft smile spread across her face as she spotted him. She walked towards him, and Kavin's face lit up with a warm smile as he waved her over.

"Thanks for letting me come with you," Mithra said, her voice filled with gratitude.

Kavin's expression turned thoughtful. "I think Yuan only agreed because he wants to keep an eye on you. He still has doubts about your involvement."

Mithra's smile never wavered. "Okay," she said, her eyes sparkling with understanding.

As they joined the team at the hotel, Rahul greeted them with a cheerful smile. "Hi Kavin, hello sister!"

Smith raised an eyebrow, and Rahul casually replied, "Yes, I've decided to start calling her sister."

Yuan intervened, his eyes fixed on Kavin. "Shall we head to the orphanage?"

Kavin nodded, his jaw set in determination. "Yeah, let's go."

೮

They arrived at the orphanage, and within minutes, they were seated in the office room, facing Aunty Jo. Kavin's voice was firm and respectful as he introduced himself. "Hello, ma'am. We are the police. Are you Aunty Jo?"

Aunty Jo's expression was serene, her eyes calm. "Yes, sir. Is there a problem?"

Kavin's response was straightforward. "We're here to investigate Zoya's case."

Aunty Jo nodded, her gaze unwavering. "Very well, let's talk." She gestured to the couch, inviting them to sit.

As they settled in, their eyes were drawn to a large photo on the wall. It depicted Zoya's parents and Zoya herself as a young girl, surrounded by a garland, symbolizing their passing. A smaller photo beside it showed a happy family, with Zoya and Zara as little girls.

Yuan's eyes narrowed slightly as he asked, "Is this Zoya?" although he already knew the answer.

Aunty Jo smiled, her expression tinged with sadness. "Yes."

Yuan's gaze lingered on the photos before turning back to Aunty Jo, his eyes clouded with doubt. "Why is there no photo of Zara?"

Aunty Jo's smile faltered, and she attempted to change the subject. "Would you like some coffee?"

Kavin declined his focus solely on the investigation. "No, thank you. Can you tell us about Zoya's death? What happened?"

Aunty Jo's face crumpled, her voice barely above a whisper. "She committed suicide."

Yuan's eyes remained skeptical. "Why? What was the reason?"

Aunty Jo's voice dropped to a whisper. "I don't know."

Kavin pressed on, his tone gentle but firm. "Who informed you that she committed suicide?"

Aunty Jo's voice cracked as she recounted the events of that fateful night. "Zoya called her parents, distraught and emotional. They were in Sicilian but rushed to Lyziden, contacting me in route. They asked me to meet Zoya at the bridge, but... but they had a car accident. Zoya's mother died on the spot. I arrived too late, and Zoya passed away two days later. The police only found her body then."

Tears streamed down Aunty Jo's face, her eyes red and puffy, but genuine in their sorrow.

Kavin's voice was soft but insistent. "What happened to Zoya's father?"

Aunty Jo's voice trembled. "He was badly injured."

Kavin pressed on, his eyes locked on hers. "Where is he now?"

Aunty Jo hesitated, her silence stretching out before she finally spoke. "Zara took him abroad for treatment."

Yuan's eyes narrowed. "Why did Zara give you this orphanage?"

Aunty Jo's gaze dropped, her voice barely above a whisper. "She didn't want to come back to Lyziden."

Yuan's eyes remained skeptical as he asked, "How do you manage this place? What's your source of income?"

Aunty Jo's response was hesitant. "We rely on donations."

Yuan's gaze intensified. "And you benefit from these donations?"

Aunty Jo nodded. "Yes, various industries and individuals contribute to our cause."

Yuan's question caught everyone off guard. "Where is Zoya?"

Aunty Jo's confusion was palpable, her brows furrowed. "What do you mean? She's dead."

Yuan's eyes locked onto hers, his eyebrows rising. "Zoya or Zara?"

Aunty Jo's tone shifted, a hint of uncertainty creeping in. "The police only found one body, and they identified it as Zoya."

Yuan's voice was laced with intrigue. "So, you also have doubts about her death?"

Aunty Jo's demeanour shifted, her eyes darkening as she suggested, "If you want the truth, perhaps you should ask the police who handled the case."

Yuan's gaze lingered, his eyes narrowing. "Why is Zara hidden, and why are there no photos of her?"

The room fell silent, the tension palpable. Yuan's voice cut through the stillness, his words laced with accusation. "Did you kill Zara for her property?"

Aunty Jo's response was laced with sarcasm, her eyes flashing with attitude. "I could say anything, just like the police claiming they found Zoya's body when maybe they just planted a fake corpse to close the case."

Kavin's voice intervened, diverting the attention. "Where is Zoya's room? We'd like to search it."

Aunty Jo's expression turned icy as she led them to Zoya's room. Inside, the space was immaculate, with colourful walls and decorative cubes. Mithra's eyes wandered, her emotions raw as she took in every detail.

As they searched the room, their eyes landed on a wall with a message that left them all stunned. The words, scribbled in a childish scrawl, seemed to leap off the surface:

❧

"Where there is love, there is fear.
Where there is fear, there is no love."

29

They found a diary in Zoya and got nothing, only a diary. So, they decided to go back, and they were with diary. Mithra's mind was still reeling from the diary's revelations, her thoughts a jumbled mix of emotions. She didn't even notice when they arrived at the hotel, her silence a testament to her inner turmoil.

Room 176 is yours, Mithra. Here's your key," Kavin said, trying to rouse her from her reverie.

But Mithra was too far gone. Her eyes glazed over as she took the key from Kavin. "Huh? Oh, sorry..." she trailed off, still lost in thought.

Rahul raised an eyebrow, concern etched on his face. "Is she okay? What's going on?"

Sultan chimed in, "I think she's still reeling from the diary. It got to her."

Rahul teased, "Oh, Sultan, can you think about anything besides the case?"

Sultan's face turned bright red as he smiled sheepishly. "Hey, someone's got to keep the theories going!"

Rahul chuckled, nudging him playfully. "Look at him, always the detective!"

The discussion turned to the mysterious circumstances of Zoya's death. Kapil's eyes narrowed; his gaze fixed on Kavin. "I think Aunty Jo is hiding something. She seems to be hinting at something more to Zoya's death."

Kavin's instincts kicked in, his mind racing with possibilities. "Yes, her words seemed laced with an underlying message. It's as if she wants us to uncover a truth that's been hidden in plain sight."

Kapil's voice took on a determined tone. "She knows something, and I aim to find out what."

Kavin's jaw set in resolve. "Lee, can you get me the case details for Zoya's death? I want to reopen the case as soon as possible."

Lee nodded, already heading for the door. "I'll get them for you. This case just got a lot more interesting."

Yuan's eyes locked onto Kavin's, seeking clarity. "What's your plan?"

Kavin's face lit up with a mix of excitement and rage. "I want to dig up her grave."

Kapil's jaw dropped; shock etched on his face. "What are you saying? That's... that's desecration!"

Kavin's stare intensified. "I need to know if Zoya's body is even in that grave. We can't trust anything at this point."

The group fell silent, digesting Kavin's words. Rahul's eyes softened as he read Zoya's diary. "She had so many dreams, so many good intentions for Mithra... it's heartbreaking."

Smith nodded in agreement. "Mithra needs to read this. She deserves to know the truth."

Yuan handed the diary over, his expression somber. "Let her read it. Maybe it'll bring some closure."

Mithra sat slumped in her chair, lost in thought, her eyes cast downward. "She hasn't written a single word about me... I'm glad she hates me. It's what I deserve."

The knock at the door broke the silence, and Mithra rose to answer it. When she opened the door, Kavin stood before her, his eyes cast down, clutching Zoya's diary. Their eyes met, and for a moment, they shared a silent understanding. "Can I hug you?", they both thought, but neither dared to bridge the gap.

"We think you should read this," Kavin said softly, offering the diary.

Mithra took it, her voice barely above a whisper. "Thank you."

Kavin nodded, sensing her emotions. "Good night," he whispered, before turning to leave.

Mithra closed the door, leaning against it for support. She slid down, her back against the door, her eyes welling up with tears as she gazed at the diary. Fear gripped her heart, but with a newfound determination, she opened the diary and began to read.

Dear Ziii,

As I stepped through the school gates on my first day, I felt an inexplicable flutter in my chest. Little did I know, fate had a surprise in store for me. That's when I saw him—the epitome of handsomeness, with eyes that rivalled the deepest ocean. My heart skipped a beat as our gazes met, and I felt like I was drowning in their depths.

But, in a moment of clumsiness, my leg twisted, and I fell. Mortification washed over me as I heard his concerned voice. "Are you okay?" His hand reached out to help me up, and our palms touched. It was as if time stood still. The world around us melted away, leaving only the two of us suspended in a sea of possibility.

His eyes, like a fish tank, held a gentle black fish that seemed to swim deeper into my soul. I felt myself getting lost in their depth, imagining a future where he'd hold my hand like a groom holds his bride's. The fantasy was shattered when he asked again, "What happened? Are you okay?"

As I gazed into his eyes, my heart raced, and my palm felt the warmth of his. He held my wrist tightly, and I felt a jolt of electricity run through me. His eyes broke contact, and I followed his gaze to my elbow, where a trickle of blood had formed. Dizziness washed over me, and I fell again, this time into the darkness of unconsciousness.

When I opened my eyes, I found myself in the school nursing room. The nurse's concerned voice asked, "Are you okay? How do you feel now?" I murmured, "I feel happy." She looked puzzled, and I quickly corrected myself, "I mean, I'm okay, thank you."

As I left the nursing room, I couldn't help but search for him. But he was nowhere to be found. I felt a pang of disappointment, wondering if I'd ever see him again. Little did I know, fate had just begun to weave its magic.

\- Zoya

ॐ

Dear Ziii

Sorry for not coming for four days. I met a girl. She was so kind I wanted to make friends with her. Do you know what made me like her, 'her smile'? Her name is Mithra.

The next day I was transferred to the other section. Her friend was in my section. She comes to see her. I like their friendship. I just want to be with them. I want to make it a trio.

God also wanted me to move to her section, and I sat beside her. It all happens like a dream. We all have a person. Probably we never met them, but we hate or like them at first sight. I like her.

I want to be a good friend. The boy's name was Kavin. We met again, so I came to his name. You like someone, nobody; it was Mithra. I don't want to be disturbed by her.

I made a mistake without her permission. I packed her things in her bag. She became angry because of me that she doesn't like anyone to touch her belongings.

- Zoya

છ

Dear Ziii,

It's all over now. Sorry for not coming for too many days. I left that school. I leave Sicilian I leave Mithra. I will leave. Mithra only knows about my phobia. I don't know how they know about me. One bully gang bullied me. They poured blood on me; no one helped except Advik. In front of Mithra, only it happens. She turns herself and leaves me just like that.

Advik, help me. He was a rich guy in our school. I thought he was kind, but I was wrong. He cheated me. The bullying gang was his friends. He pretended like his love for me and he took care of me just for time to pass. He wants to play with my feelings. The rumours are spread like I love him because of his money.

At last, the management called my parents and gave me TC. We moved to Lyziden, and now we are in Zara Orphanage. It's my dad's brother's orphanage. We are staying in our grandmother's house. It has never happened if she could be my friend. I compare her with Cube because I like both, a cube and Mithra. She is an unsolved cube...

- Zoya.

30

Dear Ziii,

Six years have passed in these six years. Many things have changed my life, my place, my wishes, my dreams, my personality, and finally my love.

I am in a relationship with Mahit. He is an artist who draws love in my heart and adds colours to my life.

I met him at Lyziden Bridge. He was looking at the. River; turned his head several times. I think he was standing there to die—to die? The day when I came to Lyziden, he was the one who welcomed me. But he never told me about that, and I didn't ask him anything about that.

We started loving each other. It felt like I was in a colourful painting. He was the artist who gave me every colour in my life.

I want to be with him, seeing him smile and looking into those eyes that were already looking into mine.

I want to be with him. Holding his hand, it felt like my heart floating in the sky like cotton.

I want to be with him. He is the one who brings colours to my black-and-white life.

Once he held my hand and said, "Fall in love, fall in love with me. Give me a chance to show what is called true love". (His black eyes are looking at me, and they never stop looking at me. I forget the place where I am standing; I forget where I am living; I only remember his eyes.) "Zoya, are you?" I blink; he breaks holding hands, but those eyes are still on me. "Zoya, take your time. I am here with you. If you understand what love is that day, I will hold your hands forever," he smiled.

Two years went by with happy memories. One day I collected my pieces of confidence and went to express my love. I saw my father talking to him. He decided to leave the orphanage, and he decided to go to university for further study. I think again I failed to understand what love is.

"Zoya, I am sorry. I want to give you a better future; I want to hold your hands forever, and I don't want your eyes to look down in shame. Believe me, I will come back if you trust me. Wait for me, he said, leaving me never speaking a word.

"Distance makes love crazy. Craziness teaches what love is,

Love makes me mad, and madness makes me see him to hold him forever."

I realize what is called love. I want to see him and express my love. So, I decided to go to his university, barely waiting to see him. The next day I got ready, and I asked permission from Dad, and he gave me the car key, and he gave me money. I decided to buy something for prose. I told everyone about this, and all gave some ideas I searched on the net.

I decided to give flowers. I went from the orphanage, and my eyes caught a flower shop. I went to buy flowers. In the flower shop, I saw people buying roses for their loved ones. It felt strange.

"How strange roses are,

It hurts the person who loves them.

How strange we are,

We express our love with the same rose."

৪৩

The flower shop lady asks, "What flower do you want?" I saw a daisy flower. Yes, I brought Gerbera daisies. I have heard that these pink daisy flowers show true love.

I went to his university. I asked other students, and coincidentally, I met his friend, Mahit, who told me everything about me and our love.

I saw Mahit under the tree. He was scrolling on his phone. He was in a dark teal colour shirt; the first time my eyes felt blush while seeing him. His friend called his name loudly. He saw me; he was shocked, and he came to me. His unblinking lashes and those killer eyes are killing me.

I felt shy and embarrassed. I never thought it could be like this. He saw the flowers I was holding; he took that I forgot that I had written a note; he saw that I tried to snatch that, but he was so strong.

He read it, 'Could you be my sun?' exactly what I had written. He asks me what it means. I have no words. He stops himself and says, "For whom you brought this." I was shocked. I don't know what to say. I forgot what language I was using. Everything in my memory was fading; my brain was not working. I took a deep breath and got courage.

"For you," I finished in one sentence. "For me why?" he asks me. I know he was teasing me. I made an angry face and turned back.

He hugs me from behind. I hold my wrist tightly; my heart skips a beat when I feel his breath in my neck. He gave a goosebump, his hand holding my waist. I tightened my lips and closed my eyes. "I told them to wait. I want to be better in front of it; it stops my every sense. "I love you." I didn't let him talk. I don't want to do that.

I expressed my love and told him why I came to him. Our eyes are filled with tears. He never took his eyes off mine. "I love you so much," he smiled, the tears flowing in his eyes. I placed my head on his. Cheats my hand, holding him. I could feel his heartbeat; it was fast. He tightly hugs me. We are closer; he too can feel my heart.

"I'm sorry to interrupt, but I have to," his friend distracts us. "What?" Mahit asks him. "If you got caught by the principal, that's it, so I plan," he wants to say something. "Make it fast." Mahit has no patience. "You can go from here. I will ensure that you have a severe fever, so you went to the hospital. Mahit hugs him; they express their friendship.

We went from there, and we had a good and lovable time. Years passed, and our love got stronger and stronger day by day.

I think my fate is bad. We love hard; we are good. I was happy with my life till he entered my life. I saw Advik in the shop. He got my phone number; he is disturbing me and saying that he loves me.

Now it has gotten worse and worse than I imagined.

- Zoya.

෮

Dear Ziii,

Ziii! I love you. You're the only person with whom I can share everything without hesitation. You're the person who never judged me. Thanks for being with me and listening to the talks. It is a last letter for you because I am a new person; from now on, I will kill everyone. Thanks, Ziii.

Love you.

Goodbye.

- Zoya.

໌

Dear Mahit

That's the love I saw in your eyes,

The love I felt in your gentle touch,

The love I experienced when I was by your side,

That's the love that makes me fearless of leaving this world, but terrified of being separated from you.

I hope you understand.

Thank you, Sun. I'm in love with the sun, which shines every day.

Goodbye.

Don't worry; I will come to meet you on the day that has no enemies.

- You're Daisy.

31

Smith's eyes locked onto Rahul as he uttered the chilling words: "I will kill everyone... I will come to meet you on the day that has no enemies." The room fell silent as if the weight of his statements had sucked the air out of it.

Rahul's voice broke the stillness, his tone laced with conviction. "We all know what this means. She's alive, and she's the one killing everyone. Zoya is the killer."

The others nodded in agreement, their faces sombre.

Yuan turned to Kavin, his voice low and urgent. "What do we do now?"

Kavin's jaw clenched. "We need to move, Sisalian. She's the target, and Zoya will come for her. We can't stay here."

"Agreed," Yuan said, glancing at his watch. "We can leave at 5:00 PM. That gives us a few hours to prepare."

Rahul stood up, his eyes scanning the room. "Alright, let's move. We have packing to do."

Kavin's gaze dropped, his eyes clouding with confusion. "I'll stay here," he said, his voice barely above a whisper.

Rahul's eyes widened in shock, his voice rising to a near shout. "What? Why? We can't leave you behind!"

Kavin's expression remained enigmatic, his words laced with a sense of foreboding. "I don't know... it feels like we're missing something. Something is hidden, just out of sight."

Kapil stepped forward, his loyalty unwavering. "I'll stay with you, Kavin."

Kavin had made his decision. "No, you need to get permission to check Zoya's grave. Time is running out—only fifteen days left. Sunaina must be careful. Sultan will stay here with me; the rest of you must go to Sisalian. Yuan, guide the team."

Yuan nodded, his eyes narrowing as he accepted the responsibility. "And follow Mithra," Kavin added, his voice low and mysterious. "Zoya will come to meet her. I'm certain of it."

As the group prepared to leave, Yuan's parting words hung in the air. "Take care, Kavin. We'll be watching from afar."

With that, they vanished into the shadows, leaving Kavin and Sultan behind. The silence was oppressive, heavy with unspoken questions. What secrets lay hidden in Lyziden? What darkness was Kavin trying to uncover? And what lay in store for Mithra, now a pawn in a deadly game?

Mithra opened the door with a soft creak, her eyes red-rimmed from crying in response to Kavin's knock. He stepped inside, his gaze locking onto hers with a quiet intensity.

"Come in," she whispered, her voice cracking as she tried to hide her sorrow.

Kavin's eyes never left hers as he entered, his face a mask of concern. He didn't ask what was wrong; he knew.

Mithra handed him Zoya's journal, her hand brushing against his. "I finished reading it," she said, her voice barely above a whisper.

Kavin took the journal, his fingers wrapping around it like a lifeline. "They're moving back to Sisalian. You need to get ready," he said, avoiding eye contact, his voice low and husky.

Mithra's eyes searched his face, seeking answers. "What about you? Why aren't you coming?"

Kavin's gaze drifted back to hers, his eyes burning with deep longing. "I have some work to complete," he said, his voice laced with a hint of sadness.

The air was thick with unspoken emotions, the silence between them was palpable. Mithra's eyes welled up with tears, but she refused to let them fall.

"Come down after getting ready," Kavin said, his voice cracking as he turned to leave.

Mithra nodded, her throat constricting. "Okay."

As Kavin reached the door, he turned back, his eyes locking onto her for one last time. Mithra didn't see him. Her gaze cast downward, but he drank in the sight of her, his heart aching with a deep longing to hold and comfort her.

He slipped out of the room, leaving Mithra alone with her tears.

As the group gathered by the car, Mithra's slender figure emerged from the doorway, her eyes locked on Kavin's with a mix of longing and trepidation. She glided towards him, her movements almost ethereal, and stopped inches from his chest.

"Take care," she whispered, her voice barely audible over the gentle hum of the engine. Her lips trembled, as if the words themselves were a fragile thing, threatening to shatter at any moment.

Without warning, Kavin's arms encircled her, pulling her close as he drew her into a gentle embrace. Mithra's body relaxed, her weight sinking into his chest as she fell against him. Her hands dangled limp, her fingers brushing against his thighs.

Kavin held her with tender ferocity, his arms cradling her as if she were a delicate flower. For a fleeting instant, they stood there, suspended in a world of their own, the tension between them dissolving into a sense of deep connection.

Mithra's face tilted upwards, her eyes drifting close as she breathed in the scent of his skin. Kavin's heart pounded in his chest, his lips inches from her forehead, as he whispered a silent promise to return to her. The world around them melting away "Few days, just a few days."

For a moment, they stood there, wrapped in each other's embrace, the tension between them palpable. Then slowly she relaxed into his hold on her arms, creeping around his waist. The ring, now a symbol of their unbroken bond, seemed to burn in his pocket.

As they stood there, the distance between them felt like an insurmountable chasm, a constant reminder of the helplessness that had been suffocating their love. The journey of life, once a shared path, had now become a solitary trek, with each step leading them further away from each other.

She took her seat in the car, never daring to look at him. "What does this love want from us, in the end?" she whispered, her voice barely audible over the wind. The car moves Sultan and Kavin sends them off.

"Where is this journey of life taking us, and what lies at the end of this path of love?" Kavin whispered. The only answer was the deafening silence, a reminder that sometimes, love isn't enough to conquer all.

As Kavin and Sultan stepped into the hotel, the air was thick with anticipation. Sultan's voice broke the silence, "What's the plan now?"

Kavin's eyes seemed to hold a secret, his gaze distant as he replied, "We need to find the missing piece of the puzzle."

Sultan's curiosity grew. "Missing puzzle? What are you talking about?"

Kavin's expression turned introspective, his thoughts swirling like a maelstrom. "Zara," he whispered, the name hanging in the air like a challenge. "We have to find out who Zara is."

The words struck Sultan like a thunderbolt, leaving him stunned and searching for a search for an answer. The silence that followed was oppressive, heavy with the weight of secrets waiting to be unearthed.

Kavin's voice cut through the stillness, his words laced with urgency. "Who is she? Why does she seem so crucial to this case? And where is she now? The question hung in the air, a tantalizing trail of breadcrumbs leading them deeper into the mystery.

Sultan's eyes narrowed, his mind racing with the implications. "questions will be thousands until we uncover the truth," he said, his voice laced with determination.

"Did anyone say where Zara is exactly?" Kavin asked, his eyes scanning the room as if searching for an answer.

"No, sir," Sultan replied, his voice firm. "No one has mentioned her location."

Kavin's gaze turned inward, his thoughts churning. "What do you think about this, Sultan?"

Sultan's expression turned thoughtful. "It's like Zara is playing hide and seek with us. She's deliberately staying hidden, leaving no trail."

Kavin's eyes snapped back to the Sultan. "You think Zara and Zoya are in this together? They're behind the murders?"

Sultan nodded. "Yes, sir. It's possible. They might be working as a team, covering each other's tracks."

Kavin's mind raced with the implications. "And no one has opened their mouth about Zara... another suspicious thing is they don't have her photo."

Sultan's eyes widened. "That's why she's escaping from us. She's a ghost, invisible and untouchable."

Kavin's jaw clenched. "Not for long, Sultan. We'll find her, and when we do, she'll pay for her crimes."

Sultan's voice broke the silence. "Sir, are we going to Zara Orphanage?"

Kavin raised an eyebrow. "What do you think? Will she come there?"

Sultan shook his head. "No, sir. I think she won't come. She's too smart for that."

Kavin nodded in agreement. "You're right. She'll anticipate our move. We need to think two steps ahead."

The game of cat and mouse continued, with Zara always elusive, always hidden. But Kavin and Sultan were determined to outsmart her, to uncover the truth behind the sinister forces driving the murders.

32

Mithra's arrival in Sisalian is met with despair; her slumped posture and downtrodden eyes betray the weight of her emotional burden. As she shuffles through her home, her luggage abandoned, her feet carry her towards the bathroom, seeking solace in the solitude of the shower.

Mithra's fragile form trembled as she stepped into the shower, the warm water enveloping her like a gentle embrace. But even its soothing touch couldn't calm the tempest raging within her. Her mind was a battleground, with guilt and pain locked in fierce combat.

Tears streamed down her face, mingling with the water, as she whispered the haunting refrain, "Because of me..." The words cut through her like a knife, each syllable a fresh wound. Her body shook, convulsed by sobs that seemed to rip her very soul apart. Anguish contorted her face; her eyes were red and swollen from crying. She felt lost, alone, and adrift in a sea of despair. The weight of her perceived mistakes crushed her, making it hard for her to breathe. Every thought was a fresh torment, and every memory was a lash that flayed her heart.

As the water continued to flow, Mithra's cries grew louder, her voice hoarse from screaming. She was a vessel overflowing with grief, her emotions raw and uncontainable. The shower became a confessional, a sanctuary where she could unleash the torrent of feelings she'd been holding back.

In this moment, Mithra was vulnerable, exposed, and utterly human. Her pain was a palpable force, reaching out to touch the hearts of those around her. It was a poignant reminder that even in our darkest moments, we are not alone and that sometimes, all it takes is a single, cathartic cry to begin the journey toward healing.

Mithra's fragile form crumpled onto the bed, her body wracked with sobs as she surrendered to the anguish that had been consuming her. The tears flowed like a river, unstoppable and unrelenting, as she mourned the shattered remnants of her heart.

Just as she seemed to be drowning in her sorrow, the shrill ring of her phone pierced the air, jolting her back to reality. With a trembling hand, she reached for the device, wiping away the tears that still streamed down her face. She took a deep breath, attempting to compose herself and do a mask of normalcy.

But as she answered the call, her voice cracked, betraying the turmoil that still ravaged her soul. She struggled to speak, her words barely above a whisper, as she tried to conceal the heartbreak that threatened to consume her.

The effort was agony, like trying to hold back a tsunami with a broken reed. Her voice trembled, her words faltered, and her heart screamed in silence, begging for release.

With each passing moment, the charade became more unbearable, the weight of her emotions crushing her. She felt like she was suffocating under the pressure of pretending to be okay and hiding the depths of her despair. And yet, she persisted, clinging to the facade of normalcy like a lifeline, even as her heart shattered into a million pieces. The tears continued to flow, silent witnesses to her anguish, as she whispered words that meant nothing, her soul screaming in silence.

Mithra's voice trembled as she finally managed to utter a faint "Hello" in response to Nithin's persistent greetings. The effort to sound normal was exhausting, but she pushed through, desperate to conceal her emotional turmoil.

Nithin's tone was laced with doubt as he asked, "Are you home?" Mithra's grip on the phone tightened, her knuckles white with tension, as she forced a calm reply, "Yes, I'm home."

The silence that followed was oppressive, punctuated only by Nithin's hesitant attempts to speak. Mithra's anxiety grew with each passing moment, her mind racing with worst-case scenarios. "What happened?" she prodded, trying to keep her tone light.

Nithin's words trailed off, leaving Mithra's imagination to fill in the blanks. "What did you think?" she pressed, her curiosity getting the better of her.

Just as Nithin seemed to be gathering his courage, Neel's voice cut in, urging him to "Tell her fast!" The sudden interruption sent Mithra's heart racing.

With a newfound sense of urgency, Nithin blurted out his confession: "I thought to express my love towards Manasvi. Please help me!" The words tumbled out in a rush, leaving Mithra stunned.

At that moment, Mithra's thoughts swirled with a mix of emotions: shock, surprise, and a hint of curiosity.

Mithra's teasing tone danced through the phone lines. "Wow? Finally, you're going to express your feelings?" Nithin's nervous laughter echoed in response: "Stop teasing me; I'm still scared to tell her my feelings."

Their shared laughter eased the tension, and Mithra's curiosity took over. "Okay, what's your plan?" Nithin's voice trembled with excitement as he revealed his strategy: "Today's the Lantern Festival, and she believes in its magic... I thought it'd be the perfect time to propose to her."

Mithra's interest was piqued. "Where did you choose? Any specific place?" Nithin's reply was laced with romance: "Hiyan Mountain. I think it'll be a beautiful backdrop for the moment."

Mithra's squeal of delight was infectious. "Wow, so romantic! What do I have to do?" Nithin's plan unfolded like a well-rehearsed script: "You ask her to come to Hiyan Mountain to celebrate the Lantern Festival. Make it seem like a friends' get-together."

Mithra's eyes narrowed. "Suddenly, how are you so confident?" she asked, sensing a shift in Nithin's behaviour.

A hint of mystery laced Nithin's response. "I'll tell you later; please be with me," he implored, his voice tinged with a hint of vulnerability.

Nithin's pleading tone, despite Mithra's curiosity, swayed her. "Okay, we'll meet in the evening," she confirmed. "Bring her sharp at 7:00," Nithin emphasized, his voice laced with anticipation.

The call ended, leaving Mithra with a warm, fuzzy feeling. She couldn't wait to play her part in Nithin's grand romantic gesture.

Nithin and Neel arrived at the mountain, their excitement palpable as they gazed up at the rooftop haven, they had chosen for the special moment. The rooftop was a flurry of activity. Zara and Aarav decorate every inch of the space with vibrant balloons, twinkling lights, and colourful flowers.

The air was electric with the spirit of friendship and camaraderie, each friend eager to contribute to Nithin's grand romantic gesture. Some were busy arranging a delectable spread of food, while others tended to the cake, adorned with intricate designs and sweet messages.

Neel, ever the grill master, was busy firing up the barbeque makers, the savoury aromas wafting through the air, teasing their taste buds. Neel and others set up stoves and cooking stations, ready for a divine feast.

As the friends worked together, their laughter and chatter filled the air, creating a joyful symphony that echoed across the mountainside. Nithin watched, his heart swelling with gratitude, as his friends transformed the rooftop into a veritable wonderland. Time flew by in a whirlwind of activity, and before long, they transformed the rooftop into a breathtakingly beautiful setting, a testament to the power of friendship and love. As they finished decorating, the friends gathered around Nithin, their faces beaming with pride and excitement.

"It's perfect!" Neel exclaimed, clapping Nithin on the back.

Nithin's eyes shone with emotion as he gazed out at the stunning setup. "You guys are the best," he said, his voice choked with gratitude.

Mithra's hushed voice whispered through the phone lines, "Hello Nithin, we've reached the spot. Where are you?" Nithin's nervousness was palpable as he replied, "Reached."

Mithra's voice was barely audible, her words laced with the thrill of surprise, "Okay, come to the roof, our friend's spot." The line went dead, leaving Nithin's heart racing with anticipation.

As Mithra led Manasvi to the rooftop, Nithin's anxiety spiked. "She came... they're coming here... what to do? I forgot everything!" he stammered, his mind blank like a student facing a surprise exam.

Neel's calm voice intervened, "No, be bold; everything will be alright." Nithin's friend offered a reassuring smile, helping to steady his nerves.

With a deep breath, Nithin steeled himself for the moment of truth. The lights were extinguished, plunging the rooftop into romantic darkness. Nithin and Neel retreated to a corner, hiding from view to allow Nithin a private moment with Manasvi.

The silence was oppressive, punctuated only by the sound of footsteps approaching. Nithin's heart pounded in his chest, his mind racing with possibilities. He took another deep breath, his eyes fixed on the spot where Manasvi would emerge from the darkness.

As Mithra and Manasvi stepped onto the rooftop, the silence was shattered by Manasvi's curious voice. "Why is this place dark and silent? No one comes here till now, right?" Her words echoed through the stillness, piercing Nithin's heart like a gentle arrow.

Mithra's response was a gentle smile as she slipped away into the darkness, leaving Manasvi alone. "Mithra, where are you going?" Manasvi called out, confusion etched in her voice.

But before she could get an answer, the lights flickered to life, bathing the rooftop in a warm, golden glow. Manasvi's eyes widened as she took in the breathtaking beauty of the setting. The flowers, the balloons, the twinkling lights—every detail was a testament to Nithin's love and devotion.

And then she saw him. Nithin stood before her, his eyes shining with nervous excitement, a bouquet trembling in his hand. His leg twisted awkwardly, betraying his anxiety, but his smile remained steadfast.

As Manasvi's gaze met Nithin's, time seemed to stand still. The world around them melted away, leaving only the two of them suspended in a moment of pure magic.

With a deep breath, Nithin took a step forward, his eyes locked on Manasvi's. He knelt, the flowers still clutched in his hand and spoke the words he had longed to say for so long...

As Nithin uttered the word "Sorry," a collective tap on the head echoed through the rooftop, a gentle reprimand for his nervous hesitation. Manasvi's soft repetition of the word "sorry" only added to the tender moment.

But Nithin's nervousness was short-lived. As he gained confidence and locked eyes with Manasvi, his gaze filled with unshed tears. His voice trembled with emotion as he poured out his heart, "I love you... will you be my half-heart and full life?"

The words struck a chord deep within Manasvi's soul, and tears of joy began to flow like a river. "Finally, you broke your barriers," she whispered, her voice trembling with happiness.

Nithin's eyes shone with tears as he caught her tears in his palm, cradling them like precious pearls. He rose to his feet, his smile radiant, and gently wiped away her tears. "Be my luck," he whispered, his voice filled with longing.

Manasvi's response was a gentle whisper. "I love you so much, my idiot." The words hung in the air like a sweet promise.

As Nithin enveloped her in a tender embrace, the rooftop seemed to fade away, leaving only the two of them lost in a sea of love and emotions. The world around them melted into a soft, golden haze as if the very universe had conspired to bring them together.

In that moment, time stood still, and all that existed was the beating of their hearts, synchronized in perfect harmony. The air was alive with the sweet scent of blooming flowers, and the soft rustle of leaves seemed to whisper secrets of love that would last an eternity.

As Nithin and Manasvi broke apart from their tender embrace, a chorus of applause erupted from the shadows. Their friends, who had been hiding in anticipation, emerged with beaming smiles, their faces radiant with happiness.

Neel, ever the jokester, was the first to reach Nithin, a mischievous glint in his eye. "Idiot," he teased, repeating Manasvi's words as he playfully ruffled Nithin's hair.

In a sudden display of affection, Neel wrapped Nithin in a tight hug. "You did well, buddy," he whispered, his voice cracking with emotion. Nithin reciprocated, and they stood there, holding each other, as tears of joy streamed down their faces.

In that instant, the bonds of friendship were palpable, a breathing entity that wrapped itself around their hearts. Laughter and tears mingled in the air as they celebrated not just Nithin's love but the unbreakable ties that bound them together.

As the emotional hug fest came to an end, Nithin's friends turned to him with curious grins. "Ok, Nithin, why did you say sorry?" they asked in unison, their eyes sparkling with amusement.

Nithin's face turned a deep shade of crimson as he looked down, his toes curling in embarrassment. "Because... I twisted my leg in nervousness," he admitted, his voice barely above a whisper. "It seemed like I spoiled the atmosphere, so I said sorry." The rooftop erupted into a fit of laughter and teasing.

As the merriment died down, it was time to leave the lanterns, a symbol of their love and friendship, to light up the night sky. With a collective sigh of happiness, they released the lanterns, watching in awe as they soared into the darkness, like tiny stars.

The romance between Nithin and Manasvi was palpable, a beautiful thing that filled their hearts with joy. As they gazed into each other's eyes, in that moment, they knew that their bond was unbreakable, a flame that would burn bright for years to come. And as they walked hand in hand,

Finally, they gathered around the table, and the dinner was served. The wind carried the sweet scent of blooming flowers, and the twinkling lights cast a magical glow on their faces. The atmosphere was enchanting, a perfect blend of warmth and wonder.

But amidst the joy and camaraderie, one heartbeat with a hint of sadness. Mithra's eyes sparkled with smiles, but her gaze often drifted away, lost in thought. Her heart missed someone, a love that was absent, yet deeply felt.

Though she didn't reveal her emotions, a subtle melancholy lingered a gentle ache that only she knew. Her friends, oblivious to her sorrow, continued to laugh and chat, their spirits high.

Mithra's mask of happiness was convincing, but the wind whispered secrets, and the lights seemed to sense her hidden truth. The shadows danced around her, a gentle reminder that even amid joy, a piece of her heart remained elsewhere, longing for a love that was yet to be.

Rachel's innocent question pierced the air, "Where is Kavin?" Mithra's heart skipped a beat as she struggled to maintain her composure. Her eyes fluttered, and her voice trembled ever so slightly as she replied, "He's handling a case."

The words felt like a fragile shield, barely concealing the turmoil brewing inside her. Rachel's response was a gentle "Ok," oblivious to the emotional storm Mithra was weathering.

As the evening wore on, Mithra's friends continued to laugh and chat, their joy infectious. She forced a smile, determined to hide her true feelings. Mithra's friends savoured the food, enjoyed the company, and let the night drift by, a gentle breeze carrying their whispered conversations.

But Mithra's heart remained elsewhere, her thoughts drifting to Kavin, wondering where he was, what he was doing, and why he wasn't there to share in the happiness. The ache within her grew, a constant reminder of the love that was absent.

As the night drew to a close, Mithra's friends bid each other farewell, their faces aglow with happiness. Mithra's mask remained intact, but the shadows knew her secret, and the wind whispered promises of a love yet to be reunited.

33

Vibha's voice trembled as she called Aarav, her colleague and friend. "Hello, Aarav," she said, trying to sound casual despite the turmoil brewing inside her.

"Hello, Vibha, where are you? I haven't seen you since morning," Aarav replied, his tone laced with concern.

Vibha hesitated, her voice barely above a whisper. "I didn't come to the hospital today... I took a leave."

Aarav's instincts kicked in, sensing something was amiss. "Where are you? Why are you speaking like this?" he asked, his doubt growing.

Vibha's response was laced with a hint of fear. "First, promise me you won't scold me."

Aarav's curiosity was piqued. "Where are you?" he asked, his tone firm but gentle.

Vibha's voice trembled further. "First, promise me..."

Aarav's gut told him something was wrong. "Did you go to the police station?" he asked, his shock evident.

Vibha's denial was quick, but her tone betrayed her. "No..."

Aarav's concern turned into anger. "Then what? Why are you hiding something from me?"

Vibha's voice cracked as she revealed the truth. "We came to Harsha's home..."

Aarav's shock turned into fear. "What? Why did you go there?"

Vibha tried to console him, but her words only fueled his anger. "I'm not alone... Riya is with me."

Aarav's questions came on rapid-fire. "Who else is there? Are you inside the house?"

Vibha's responses were laced with fear, her voice barely audible. "Just us two... Yes, we're inside."

Aarav's anger boiled over, his concern for Vibha's safety overriding his emotions. "You... How could you be so reckless?"

Vibha's innocent tone cut through Aarav's anger. "Aarav, can you please come here? It's quite scary..."

Aarav's protective instincts took over. "Send me the location."

Vibha's response was hesitant, but she knew she had no choice. "It's near the hospital..."

Aarav's anger returned, mixed with fear. "Wait, I'll come and... I'll come to get you."

Aarav's phone buzzed with the location message, and he couldn't help but mutter under his breath, "This girl..." His concern for Vibha's safety had turned to frustration, mixed with a hint of anger.

Without hesitation, he approached his chief, requesting half-day permission. The chief, aware of the current calm in the hospital, granted the request. Aarav wasted no time, jumping into his car and speeding towards the location.

As he arrived, he called Vibha, his voice firm but laced with worry. "I'm here. Where are you?"

Vibha's response was barely above a whisper. "Come inside..."

Aarav's heart raced as he stepped out of the car and approached the house. The silence was oppressive, and the atmosphere sent shivers down his spine. He pushed open the creaky door, his eyes scanning the dimly lit interior.

The house seemed to swallow him whole, its silence a living entity that wrapped around him like a shroud. Aarav's instincts screamed at him to be cautious, but his concern for Vibha drove him forward.

"Vibha?" he called out, his voice low and steady.

The only response was the creaking of the old wooden floorboards beneath his feet. Aarav's heart pounded in his chest as he ventured deeper into the house, his senses on high alert. Where was Vibha?

Aarav's heart skipped a beat as he ventured deeper into the house, his senses on high alert. Suddenly, a gentle tap on his shoulder made him jump, his fear momentarily getting the better of him. He spun around, ready to face the unknown, but was met with Vibha's mischievous grin.

"It's me," she whispered, her eyes sparkling with a mix of fear and excitement.

Aarav's relief quickly turned to annoyance, and he folded her ear, a gentle punishment for scaring him half to death. "Ahhh!" Vibha screamed, more in surprise than pain.

"Did you find something?" Aarav asked, his voice was low and urgent.

Vibha rubbed her sore ear. "We came just a few minutes ago, and I called you immediately."

Aarav's expression softened. "At least you called me now. Where's Riya?"

Vibha nodded towards the hallway, "She's upstairs. Come, let's go."

As they spoke, the creaking of floorboards echoed through the hallway, suspicious sounds that made Aarav's instincts scream a warning. He quickly dragged Vibha into the nearby cupboard, his heart racing with anticipation.

The cupboard was cramped, the air thick with dust and secrets. Aarav's eyes locked onto Vibha's, his gaze intense. "Shh, someone's coming," he whispered, his voice barely audible.

Vibha's eyes widened, her breath catching in her throat. They waited, frozen in silence, as the footsteps drew closer...

In the cramped cupboard, Aarav and Vibha's bodies were pressed together, their chests touching, sending sparks flying through Aarav's veins. Vibha, however, seemed oblivious to the proximity, her gaze avoiding his, her expression casual.

But Aarav was transfixed, his eyes locked onto hers, his heart racing like a volcano about to erupt. He could feel Vibha's heartbeat, sense her very being, and it was intoxicating.

As they stood there, frozen in time, Aarav realized his hand was grasping Vibha's shoulder, his fingers digging into her skin. He jerked it back as if burned.

Vibha, meanwhile, peeked through a small gap in the cupboard, her eyes scanning the hallway. But instead of danger, she saw Riya, standing alone, looking puzzled.

Vibha turned back to Aarav, her eyes narrowing, her expression a mix of disappointment and curiosity. Aarav, still reeling from their proximity, was shocked, his hand instinctively reaching for hers.

But Vibha's words stopped him from cold. "It was Riya."

Aarav's hand dropped, his face flushing with embarrassment. Riya, oblivious to the drama, looked on, confusion etched on her face.

The tension was palpable, the air thick with unspoken emotions. Aarav's heart still raced, his feelings for Vibha threatening to spill over. But he pushed them back, unsure of how to process the maelstrom of emotions swirling inside him.

Vibha's voice was laced with a sense of urgency, "Let's go to his room and search." Aarav nodded in agreement, his eyes still locked onto hers, but he quickly looked away, not wanting to reveal his true feelings.

As they entered Harsha's room, a sense of unease settled over them. The air was thick with the scent of decay, and the broken flower vase on the floor seemed to scream violence. Vibha's eyes widened as she spotted the bloodstain on the shattered glass.

Aarav instinctively stopped her from touching the glass, his bare hands closing around the shard. Vibha's heart skipped a beat as she watched him, concern etched on her face.

But Vibha was prepared, her eyes scanning the room for any other clues. She pulled out small covers, and Aarav carefully placed the blood-stained glass inside. Vibha's gaze fell upon the medicines scattered on the table, her eyes widening as she read the labels. "These are depression drugs," she whispered.

Aarav's shock was palpable, his voice barely above a whisper. "What?"

Vibha's hands moved swiftly, collecting every sample, every shred of evidence. They searched the room thoroughly, unearthing documents and papers belonging to Harsha's work. But it was the scribbled notes that made their blood run cold. "Sorry, please leave me..." and "I will kill you..." The words seemed to sear themselves into their minds.

Aarav's voice was low and urgent, "Let's get out of here. Something's not right."

Vibha understood, her eyes locking onto him. They quickly gathered every shred of evidence, their hearts racing with a sense of foreboding. As they left the room, the silence between them was oppressive, heavy with unspoken fears.

Riya's eyes welled up with tears, her body shaking uncontrollably as she whispered, "It seems someone murdered him." The words hung in the air like a dark cloud, casting a shadow of fear over the group.

Vibha's expression was soft, her voice gentle as she consoled Riya. "Please stay calm; we'll get through this." But the reassurance seemed to fall flat, as Riya's tears continued to flow.

As they left the house, the weight of their discovery settled heavily on their shoulders. The silence between them was oppressive, punctuated only by Riya's sniffles.

When they reached Riya's home, Vibha's words were laced with compassion. "Look, don't be scared; we're right behind you. I'll inform you if anything happens." But Riya's eyes betrayed her fear, her mind racing with the gruesome truth.

As they bid Riya farewell, Aarav and Vibha exchanged a knowing glance. The hospital was their next destination, where they would unravel the mysteries of Harsha's death. The darkness of the night seemed to swallow them whole as they drove towards the hospital, their hearts heavy with foreboding.

Vibha ran to the lab; after some minutes, she came out of the lab, a look of anticipation on her face. Aarav's eyes met hers, his voice tinged with curiosity. "What happened?"

Vibha's response was matter-of-fact. "She told us to come back when the report is ready; she'll call us." Vibha took help from her friend who works in medical laboratory technology.

Aarav nodded, his expression practical. "Ok, let's go and do our work."

Vibha's goodbye was brief: "Ok, bye." But as she turned to leave, Aarav's voice stopped her.

"Vibha."

She turned back, expecting him to say something, but Aarav's lips remained sealed. Vibha's eyebrows rose, her eyes questioning.

Aarav's voice was barely audible, "Nothing."

He turned and walked away, leaving Vibha puzzled. But as she watched him go, a smile spread across her face. Her mind began to wander, filled with the memory of their touch in the cupboard. Her imagination ran wild, replaying the moment their chests had touched, the spark that had flown between them.

Vibha's cheeks flushed, her heart racing with a newfound awareness. She turned and walked away, her steps light, her mind lost in the possibilities.

34

Kavin approached Sultan, a cup of steaming coffee in hand, and offered it to him with a nod. "Sultan, have it."

Sultan's eyes widened in surprise, but he quickly masked it with a nod of respect. "Sir, why did you bring it?" he asked, his voice laced with gratitude.

Kavin's expression remained stoic, his voice firm. "We've received orders to exhume Zoya's grave. We need to be sharp."

With the coffee accepted, they set out to fulfil their duty. The police force of Lyziden converged on the graveyard, their footsteps echoing through the stillness. One officer began to dig, the sound of the shovel hitting the earth a stark contrast to the silence.

As they lifted the coffin from the grave, a collective breath was held. But when they opened the box, shockwaves rippled through the team. The coffin was empty, a chilling void where Zoya's body should have lain.

The implications were dire. Kavin's eyes narrowed, his mind racing. "Who handled this case?" he demanded, his voice low and urgent.

Lee hesitated, his eyes darting around the team. "It was handled by the chief, sir," he replied, his voice laced with a hint of unease.

Kavin's gaze pinned him. "Make a call, Mr. Lee. We need answers now."

Lee nodded, his fingers flying across his phone's keypad. The air was thick with tension as he waited for an answer, the team's eyes fixed on him with a mix of anticipation and trepidation.

Finally, Lee spoke, his voice low and urgent. "Chief, we have a problem. The coffin is empty... Yes, sir... I understand... Right away, sir."

The team exchanged uneasy glances, the silence oppressive. Kavin's eyes never left Lee's face, his expression a mask of determination. The investigation had just taken a dark and unexpected turn.

Kavin's voice was firm as he spoke to the chief. "You know what we're dealing with now."

The chief's response was curt. "Yes."

"Did you find Zoya's body at the bridge?" Kavin pressed on, his eyes narrowing.

"Yes, we did," the chief replied, his tone steady.

Kavin's anger flared, but he kept it in check. "Lie. There's no dead body."

The chief's expression remained impassive. "The order came from a higher official."

Kavin's attitude turned defiant. "Can I meet this higher official?"

The chief's voice was detached. "You can request an appointment through their office."

Kavin's eyes flashed with determination. He knew he was being stonewalled, but he was determined to uncover the truth.

Kavin's eyes were lost in thought as he instructed Sultan, "Arrange a meeting with that higher official."

Sultan nodded, accepting the task. "Ok, sir."

The two men departed, their minds preoccupied with the mysterious case. Hours passed before the Sultan returned, his expression hesitant.

"Sir, I've arranged the meeting, but..." Sultan's voice trailed off, his sentence unfinished.

Kavin's gaze snapped back to him, his eyes narrowing. "But what? Why are you dragging this out?"

Sultan took a deep breath before completing his sentence. "The higher official is busy, and their schedule is tight. They've agreed to meet you tomorrow."

Kavin's face contorted in a mixture of tension and confusion. "Tomorrow? What do you mean?"

Sultan's voice was laced with apology. "Yes, sir. Tomorrow at lunch. They've set the meeting at *The Classic Table restaurant.*"

Kavin's expression turned thoughtful, his mind racing with possibilities. "Ok."

Sultan's eyes darted around the people before focusing on Kavin. "Sir, it seems Advik's dad is behind this."

Kavin's gaze locked onto Sultan's, his eyes burning with intensity. The plot was thickening, and he was determined to uncover the truth.

"Let's head to the Zara Orphanage," Kavin said, his mind racing with possibilities.

Sultan nodded in agreement. "Ok, let's go."

Without wasting another moment, they made their way to the orphanage. Upon arrival, they entered the front office, where Aunty Jo sat casually behind the desk.

"Aunty Jo, may I come in?" Kavin asked, knocking once on the doorframe.

"Come in, Mr Kavin," Aunty Jo replied, her tone suggesting she had anticipated his visit.

Kavin's eyes narrowed as he approached her. "Why did no one attend the funeral at the graveyard?"

Aunty Jo's response was evasive. "Nothing was there, right?"

Kavin's gaze intensified. "So, you expected me to come here?"

Aunty Jo's smile was laced with attitude. "We expected you, Mr. Kavin."

Kavin's voice was low and even. "Zara, right?"

Aunty Jo's eyes sparkled with amusement. "Mmm, smart," she said, her voice dripping with sarcasm.

She reached for her phone and dialled a number, her movements swift and deliberate. Once connected, she handed the phone to Kavin.

"Hello?" Kavin said, his voice laced with curiosity.

"Hi, Kavin," a female voice replied, her tone confident and playful.

"Zara?" Kavin asked, his mind racing with possibilities.

The woman on the other end chuckled. "Yeah, don't you recognize who I am?"

Kavin's confusion deepened; he ventured, his voice uncertain. The air was charged with tension as Kavin's eyes locked onto Aunty Jo's, his mind reeling with the implications.

But before he could even finish the sentence, a simultaneous

"RACHEL!"

Burst forth from both Kavin and the mysterious woman, their voices entwining in a moment of electrifying revelation.

35

Kavin's voice was laced with a mix of confusion and urgency as he spoke to Yuan over the phone. "Hello Yuan, we dug up Zoya's grave today, but there's nothing there."

Yuan's response was immediate, his jaw dropping in shock. "What do you mean, nothing?"

Kavin's next revelation only added to Yuan's astonishment. "And there's something else. We found out who Zara is."

Yuan's excitement in his voice. "Who is she?"

Kavin's pause was deliberate, building suspense before the bombshell. "She's right in front of us, near me."

Yuan's voice dropped to a whisper, his mind racing with possibilities. "Who?"

Kavin's words were like a punch to the gut. "Rachel. She's our friend, Yuan."

Yuan's shock was still evident, his voice laced with disbelief. "What? Really?"

Kavin's explanation only added to the complexity. "She's been living with a fake identity, Yuan. We had no idea."

The silence that followed was oppressive, heavy with the weight of secrets and lies. Yuan's mind reeled, trying to process the truth about Rachel.

Kavin's voice was laced with concern as he instructed Yuan, "Mithra doesn't know about this yet, so please go check on her and make sure she's okay."

Yuan's response was immediate, his tone firm with duty. "Okay, don't worry, I'll go check on her now." Yuan's curiosity was piqued. "What are you going to do, Kavin?"

Kavin's determination was evident. "I have a meeting with a higher official tomorrow. I'll update you on what happens."

Yuan's voice was firm, his mind racing with the implications. "Can you send me a photo of Rachel?"

Kavin's response was immediate, his determination evident. "Okay, I'll send it to you right now. And inform the team about this too."

With that, Kavin ended the call, his fingers flying across the screen as he sent the photo to Yuan. The image of Rachel's smiling face, once a familiar and welcoming sight, now seemed sinister, a mask hiding a web of lies.

Yuan's words dropped like a bombshell, leaving the team stunned. "What?" Kapil asked, his voice laced with shock.

Yuan's nod was solemn, his expression grim. "Yes," he said, holding up his phone to display Rachel's photo.

The team's gasps were audible, their faces reflecting their disbelief. Rahul's confusion turned into outrage. "Then why do we have to wait? Let's arrest her!"

Yuan's caution was evident. "Do we have evidence?"

Rahul's frustration was palpable. "Ahh, she played the game well."

Smith's eyes narrowed, his mind racing. "She's missing, puzzled."

Yuan's decision was swift. "Okay, I have to go to Mithra's street to check whether she's there or not."

With that, Yuan turned to leave, his team's worried glances following him out the door. The investigation had taken a dark and unexpected turn.

As he walked, Yuan's thoughts were consumed by the enigmatic Rachel, her secrets and lies weaving a complex web that threatened to entangle them all.

Yuan's phone flashed with Mithra's address, and he swiftly moved to head out. But before he could take a step, Rahul and Smith appeared, their faces etched with a mix of concern and determination.

"What's happened?" Yuan asked, his curiosity piqued.

Rahul's expression turned grave. "We don't have any concrete evidence, so we need to search for it. And for that, we have to follow Rachel."

Smith nodded in agreement. "We should track Rachel's movements, so we called Kavin to send her address."

Just as Rahul finished speaking, his phone buzzed with an incoming message. He glanced at the screen, and his eyes widened. "It's Rachel's address."

Without hesitation, the trio sprang into action. Yuan headed to watch over Mithra, while Rahul and Smith set out to keep tabs on Rachel.

Yuan arrived at Mithra's street, keeping a safe distance to avoid detection. From his vantage point, he could see her house, and his trained eyes scanned the premises for any signs of trouble.

Their mission was to keep Mithra safe without alerting her to Kavin's concerns. Yuan's priority was to confirm her well-being without being seen.

With his eyes fixed on the house, Yuan made a call to Kavin. "Kavin, Mithra is alright. I'm at her street, watching her place."

Kavin's voice was laced with tension. "Can you see her?"

"Yes, she's okay," Yuan replied, his voice low and steady. "There's no problem. I can see her.

She's just closed the outside door and turned off every light. She's gone inside."

Yuan's gaze remained fixed on the house, his senses on high alert, ready to respond to any change in the situation.

"Thank you so much," Kavin said, his voice filled with gratitude.

Yuan hadn't finished speaking, but Kavin cut him off, his tone suddenly curt. "Yuan, you can go now. Take a rest."

Yuan sensed a hint of jealousy in Kavin's voice and smiled knowingly. "Ok, bye," he replied, his tone light and understanding.

୫৩

As Vibha's phone buzzed, she couldn't help but feel a flutter in her chest. She saw Aarav's name on the screen, and her heart skipped a beat. She took a deep breath and answered, trying to sound nonchalant.

"Aarav," she said, her voice barely above a whisper.

"Vibha, we'll meet tomorrow. I have a plan," Aarav said, his voice laced with excitement. "A weekend plan," he added, his tone hinting at adventure.

Vibha's curiosity was piqued. "Oh, okay," she replied, trying to sound casual despite her growing interest.

"Has your friend contacted you?" Aarav asked, his voice tinged with concern.

Vibha hesitated for a moment before responding, "No, she said she'll send the report via message."

Aarav's response was brief: "Oh, okay."

Vibha felt the need to reassure him. "Don't worry, I'll send it to you as soon as she sends it."

The conversation ended abruptly, but the silence that followed spoke volumes. Both Vibha and Aarav were lost in thought, their minds replaying the incident that had left them shy and happy.

They hid their true feelings behind a veil of normalcy, but the underlying tension was palpable.

As they went their separate ways, the anticipation of their weekend plan hung in the air, leaving them both wondering what tomorrow would bring.

౷

Rahul and Smith arrived at Rachel's street, maintaining a discreet distance as they surveilled her house. From their vantage point, they could see that she was indeed inside. They confirmed that all escape routes were covered, and with a sense of satisfaction, they settled in for a long night of watching.

As the hours passed, their eyelids grew heavy, and despite their best efforts, they eventually succumbed to exhaustion. The darkness and silence of the night enveloped them, and they fell into a deep sleep, unaware of the events that would soon unfold.

The next morning, Smith shook Rahul awake, his voice laced with urgency. "Rahul, wake up! We can't lose her!"

Rahul's eyes snapped open, and he sat up with a start. He rubbed the sleep from his eyes, his mind racing with the sudden realization that they might have let their guard down.

As they looked towards Rachel's house, their hearts sank. The front door was open.

Just as they were about to give up hope, a figure emerged from Rachel's house, clad in a hoodie and attempting to flee. Rahul and Smith sprang into action, their instincts on high alert.

"Go, go, go!" Smith yelled as they sprinted towards their car.

Rahul peeled out of the parking spot, and they took off in a hot pursuit, their tyres screeching as they sped through the streets. The hooded figure darted through traffic, but Rahul and Smith were hot on their heels, their adrenaline pumping with every twist and turn.

As they closed in on the car, Rahul and Smith were certain they had finally cornered Rachel. The high-speed chase had all the makings of a Hollywood blockbuster, with screeching tyres, sharp turns, and a dash of adrenaline-fueled excitement.

Finally, they managed to block the car's path and apprehend the driver. But as they approached the vehicle, their triumphant grins faltered. The person behind the wheel was not Rachel, but a clever decoy.

Their shock and confusion were palpable as they realized they had been outsmarted. The real Rachel was still at large, and they were back to square one.

Rachel had masterfully played a diversionary tactic, using the decoy to throw Rahul and Smith off her trail. The two investigators realized, too late, that they had fallen prey to her cunning plan.

With renewed urgency, Rahul and Smith sped back to Rachel's last known location, but they arrived to find Rachel had flown the coop, leaving behind only the faintest whisper of her presence.

Her escape was a testament to her cleverness and resourcefulness, leaving Rahul and Smith to regroup and reassess their strategy. The game of cat and mouse had just reached a whole new level.

36

As the morning sun cast its warm rays on Vibha's face, she woke up with a start, the memories of the previous day's incident still fresh in her mind. She couldn't shake off the feeling of shyness that lingered, a gentle reminder of the unspoken emotions between her and Aarav. But little did she know, their weekend plan was about to take a drastic turn.

Vibha's hands trembled as she reached for her phone, her heart racing with anticipation. She had been waiting for her friend's message, and finally, the report was in. With bated breath, she opened the file and began to read.

The words blurred together on the screen as her eyes widened in shock. Confusion and disbelief wrestled for dominance on her face. She felt like she had been punched in the gut, her breath knocked out of her.

With shaking fingers, she dialed Aarav's number, her voice barely above a whisper when he answered.

"Aarav... Aarav..." she stammered, her tone laced with fear and uncertainty.

Aarav's voice was laced with concern, "Vibha, what's wrong? You sound scared."

Vibha's words tumbled out in a rush, "Aarav, Harsha has been murdered..."

The line went silent, the only sound being Vibha's ragged breathing. Aarav's voice was frozen in shock, his mind struggling to process the devastating news. The weekend plan, the shy feelings, everything faded into the background as the harsh reality set in.

"Okay, don't worry; I'll come to your home." The calmness in his tone was a beacon of hope, a promise of safety.

Vibha's response was laced with desperation, "Haan, okay, come fast..." Her voice trailed off, consumed by fear. The phone slipped from her trembling hands, the call ending abruptly.

Vibha's world was turned upside down. The news of Harsha's murder had left her reeling, her mind struggling to comprehend the brutal reality. She felt like she was drowning in a sea of uncertainty, unable to find a lifeline.

As the doorbell pierced the air, Vibha's heart skipped a beat. She hesitated for a moment, her fear momentarily paralyzing her. But then she heard Aarav's voice, a gentle whisper that seemed to carry on the wind, "Vibha..."

With a surge of relief, she flung open the door and hurled herself into Aarav's arms. Tears of fear and anxiety streamed down her face as she clung to him,

Aarav's arms enveloped her, a haven from the storm raging within. "Vibha, what happened? Tell me what happened," he coaxed, his voice a soothing balm to her frazzled nerves.

As she pulled away, Vibha's eyes met Aarav's, and she saw her fear reflected on her. His eyes were red-rimmed, his face etched with concern.

"What happened?" Aarav asked again, his voice was barely above a whisper.

Vibha took a deep breath, trying to calm her racing heart. "Come in," she said, stepping aside to let him enter. "My friend sent the report..."

As Aarav's eyes scanned the report, his face transformed from concern to shock. His jaw dropped, and his lips parted in disbelief. He felt like he had been punched in the gut, the air knocked out of him.

Vibha's eyes met his, and she nodded solemnly as if confirming the worst. Aarav's gaze lingered on her face, searching for any glimmer of hope but finding none.

He took a deep breath, trying to calm himself down. His mind was racing; he knew he had to act fast. "I'll call our friends to come here," he said, his voice firm, resolute.

Vibha's response was barely audible, a faint "Ok" that spoke volumes of her trust in him. Aarav's fingers flew across his phone's screen, dialing numbers and sending messages. His movements were swift and purposeful, a stark contrast to the turmoil brewing inside him.

As he worked, Vibha's eyes never left his face, her gaze a silent plea for comfort, for reassurance. Aarav's expression softened, his eyes locking onto hers, a promise of support, of protection.

In that moment, time stood still. The world outside receded, leaving only the two of them,

Aarav's thumbs flew across his phone's screen, sending out a distress signal to their closest friends. "I've called Nithin, Neel, Manasvi, and Mithra," he told Vibha, his voice steady. "They'll be here soon. We'll discuss this with them."

Vibha nodded, her eyes still haunted by the revelation. "OK," she whispered, her voice barely audible.

Aarav's gaze softened as he turned to her. "Why are you so scared? You're a brave girl, Vibha," he said, his tone gentle.

Vibha's shoulders slumped, her body language screaming vulnerability. "It was a planned murder...I never expected it. And he took the wrong medicine..." Her voice trailed off, the words hanging in the air like a challenge.

Aarav's expression turned sympathetic. "OK, don't worry," he consoled her, his voice a soothing balm. "We'll get through this together."

Vibha's eyes dropped, her gaze fixed on the floor. "I know I reacted more...I just can't believe it," she admitted, her voice laced with self-doubt.

As the group of friends assembled in Vibha's living room, Aarav took on the role of host, introducing Vibha to the others with a warm smile. But before he could even finish, Neel's mischievous grin broke through, "Aarav, you didn't tell us you had a girlfriend!"

Vibha's cheeks flushed, and she couldn't help but smile at Neel's teasing. Aarav, on the other hand, looked sheepish, his eyes darting to Vibha before quickly looking away, a faint blush creeping up his neck.

"Hey, focus, guys!" Aarav said, trying to steer the conversation back on track. "I called you here to discuss a case."

Nithin's confusion was palpable. "Case? What case?"

Aarav nodded, gesturing for everyone to take a seat. "Yes, let's sit down and talk. It's about Harsha's murder."

The room fell silent, the lighthearted banter replaced by a somber mood.

Aarav's words hung in the air like a challenge: "Harsha was murdered with the poison cyanide." He paused, collecting his thoughts before continuing, "He was taking multiple drugs as medication, which led to hallucinations. It's possible he tried to kill himself."

The room fell silent, the weight of Aarav's words sinking in. But before anyone could process it, Vibha added a chilling detail, "And that's why he sometimes behaved with a different personality."

The group's eyes widened in shock, their faces pale. Neel's mouth dropped open, Nithin's eyes bulged, and Mithra's hands flew to her mouth. The revelation was too much to take in.

"Cyanide? Hallucinations? Different personality?" Neel stammered, trying to wrap his head around the information.

Aarav's eyes scanned the room, his gaze meeting each of his friends. "We need to go to Harsha's home for more information. Will you guys help us?"

Mithra sprang to her feet, her determination evident. "What's the question? Let's go!" she exclaimed, her voice firm.

Nithin and Neel exchanged a glance, then nodded in unison. "We're in," Nithin said, his voice resolute.

Neel stood up, his eyes flashing with excitement. "Let's do this. We owe it to Harsha to uncover the truth."

Vibha smiled, a hint of gratitude on her face. "Thank you, guys. Let's go."

With a united sense of purpose, the group filed out of Vibha's home, ready to face whatever lay ahead.

37

As they stepped into Harsha's home, an eerie silence enveloped them, like a shroud of despair. The air was heavy with an unsettling stillness, punctuated only by the faint creaks and groans of the old house. The group exchanged nervous glances, their hearts racing with anticipation.

Vibha led the way, her footsteps echoing through the deserted halls. Each step seemed to amplify the sense of foreboding as if they were being watched by unseen eyes. Aarav followed closely, his senses on high alert, scanning every nook and cranny for any sign of disturbance.

Mithra and Nithin trailed behind, their whispers barely audible, "Do you think we'll find anything?" "I don't know, but I have a bad feeling."

Vibha pushed open a door with a deep breath, and they began their search, their movements slow and deliberate, as if afraid to disturb the secrets that lay hidden within Harsha's home. The silence was oppressive, weighing heavily on their shoulders, making each step feel like a journey into the heart of darkness.

As they entered Harsha's room, a sense of nostalgia washed over them. Everything was just as they had left it, frozen in time. The bed, unmade, with the same rumpled sheets, the desk.

Nithin and Neel began to sift through the documents on the desk, their eyes scanning the pages with a mixture of curiosity and trepidation. Vibha and Aarav searched the room, their gazes sweeping every corner as if searching for a ghost.

Mithra saw the scribbles. Suddenly, a shrill ringtone pierced the air, making everyone jump. Mithra let out a startled "Ouch!" as she fumbled for her phone.

The room fell silent, all eyes on Mithra as she stared at the screen. Her expression changed from fear to surprise and then to a mix of emotions. "It's Kavin," she whispered.

She answered the call, "Kavin, what's wrong? You sound scared."

"Where are you? Are you okay?" Kavin's voice was laced with fear, his words tumbling out in a rush.

Mithra's eyes widened as she listened, her grip on the phone tightening. "What happened, Kavin? Why are you asking me all these questions?"

"Are you with Rachel?" Kavin's question was abrupt, his tone suspicious.

Mithra's confusion deepened. "No, I'm not with Rachel. Why are you asking about her?"

Kavin's pause was palpable as if he was choosing his words carefully. "Do you remember that enigmatic person, Zara, in the case? Zoya's sister?"

Mithra's brow furrowed as she tried to recall. "Oh, yes... I remember."

Kavin's next question sent a shiver down her spine. "Do you have any idea who she is?"

Mithra's confusion turned to bewilderment. "Who is she?" she asked, her voice barely above a whisper.

The silence that followed was oppressive and heavy with foreboding. Then, Kavin's words dropped like a bombshell: "Rachel."

&

Mithra's eyes widened in shock, her voice echoing through the room, "WHAT?"

The others stared at her, their faces mirroring her shock and confusion.

Mithra's world came crashing down around her as Kavin's words confirmed her worst fears. "Yes, she is Zara," he said, his voice firm and resolute.

Mithra's mind reeled, her thoughts tangled in a web of confusion and shock. She tried to speak, but her voice caught in her throat. "How...she..." she stuttered, unable to form coherent words.

Kavin's voice grew distant, his name echoing through the phone as he called out to her. "Mithra? Mithra, are you there?"

But Mithra was gone, lost in a sea of stunned silence. Neel's concerned voice cut through the fog, "Hey, what happened, Mithra?"

Neel gently took the phone from Mithra's limp hand and spoke to Kavin. "Hello, Kavin, it's Neel."

Kavin's tense voice crackled through the line. "Neel, are you there? What happened to Mithra? Why isn't she answering?"

Neel's calm demeanor soothed the situation. "Don't worry, Kavin. She's just... stunned. She's sitting down, trying to process everything. She'll be okay.

Kavin's relief was palpable. "Okay, take care of her. I'll come soon."

Neel ended the call and turned to Mithra, who still sat frozen, her eyes vacant and unseeing. The room seemed to hold its breath, waiting for her to shatter the silence.

But Mithra remained still, lost in a world of her own, as the truth about Rachel and Zara swirled around her like a vortex, pulling her under.

Nithin's gentle voice broke the silence, "What happened, Mithra? You look like you've seen a ghost."

Vibha's soothing words followed, "Take a deep breath, Mithra. Relax."

Mithra's gaze drifted towards Vibha, her eyes unfocused. Vibha's calm demeanor was a balm to her frazzled nerves. "Relax, look here," Vibha said, guiding Mithra's gaze to a point in front of her.

Mithra's voice trembled, her eyes brimming with tears. "Rachel...Rachel cheated us with her fake identity."

Manasvi's eyes widened in shock, her voice barely above a whisper. "What?"

Mithra's gaze deepened, her lips quivering. "The Sisalian serial killer case... Kavin was handling it, and Zara was the only killer."

Neel's confusion was palpable, his brow furrowed. "Rachel? Zara?"

Mithra took a deep breath, her words spilling out in a rush. "Wait, let me explain everything."

As Mithra began to unravel the tangled threads of the case, her friends listened in stunned silence. The room seemed to shrink, the air thickening with tension.

"Rachel, our friend, was Zara, the serial killer," Mithra revealed, her voice cracking. "She manipulated us, played us like pawns in her twisted game."

The team's gasps were audible, their faces reflecting their horror. Mithra's words continued to flow, each revelation more shocking than the last. The room seemed to spin as if the very foundations of their reality had been shattered.

Manasvi's voice trembled, "Zoya also?"

Mithra's nod was almost imperceptible, her eyes welling up with tears. "Yes."

Mithra's murmur was barely audible, her voice cracking with emotion. "I'm the one who's responsible for this. She became like this because of me."

Vibha and Manasvi rushed to console her, their voices soft and soothing. "No, Mithra, you did nothing wrong."

But Mithra's gaze was lost in the past, her mind consumed by memories of their school days. "No, the way she looked at me that day...I still remember."

As Mithra's words flowed, the room was transported to a different time, a different place. The team listened, entranced, as Mithra recounted the events that had shaped Zoya's destiny.

Manasvi's arms enveloped Mithra in a warm hug. "It was a mistake, Mithra. You didn't do anything intentionally."

Neel's murmur was barely audible, but it sent a ripple through the group. "Zara Orphanage."

Mithra's eyes widened in shock, her voice trembling. "Zara Orphanage?"

Neel's nod was solemn, his hand holding up a document. "Yes, the funds have been transferred."

The room fell silent as Neel revealed the shocking truth. Harsha's bank balance had been transferred to Zara Orphanage. The team's eyes scanned the document, their minds reeling with the implications.

Aarav's voice broke the silence, his words hanging in the air like a challenge. "So, Zoya and Zara have murdered Harsha."

The room seemed to spin, the team's faces reflecting their horror and confusion. Mithra's eyes welled up with tears, Manasvi's grip on her tightened, and Neel's face turned ashen. The truth was slowly unravelling.

38

Kavin adjusted his tie, his mind racing with the implications of the case. He was about to meet with the higher officials of Lyziden, and he needed to be prepared. Sultan and Lee flanked him, their expressions somber.

As they arrived at The Classic Restaurant, a sense of unease settled over Kavin. This was it—the moment of truth. Inside, they were led to a VIP room, the door closing behind them with a soft click. The officer, a tall, imposing figure, greeted them with a nod.

"Please, gentlemen, have a seat. Lunch has been ordered for you as well."

Kavin's eyes scanned the room, taking in the lavish decor and the stern faces of the officials.

The officer's voice was laced with condescension, his attitude dripping with superiority. "What do you want to say? You have half an hour."

Kavin's gaze locked onto the officer's, his eyes flashing with determination. "I'll get straight to the point. Where is Zoya's body?"

The officer's smirk grew wider, his tone dripping with menace. "You're young blood; that's why you're so reckless. Listen, behind this case are big officials, like me. So, step away from this and forget about it. What will you do with that dead body, anyway?

It's been two years, and all that's left is a skeleton."

Kavin's eyes narrowed, his voice taking on a sharp edge. "Did you find her body or not?"

The officer shifted uncomfortably, his words spilling out in a rush. "She attempted suicide at Lyziden Bridge."

Kavin pounced on the evasion, his words mirroring the officer's earlier tone. "Found or not, please, sir, I have no more time."

The officer's face reddened, his voice rising. "No, we didn't find it." eyes flashed with anger, his challenge, "You think you can find."

Kavin's nod was curt, his determination evident. "I will find what you couldn't."

Kavin stormed out of the restaurant, his footsteps echoing through the hallway. The officer's face remained tense, his eyes fixed on the door as if expecting Kavin to return.

Aarav's urgent voice crackled over the phone line. "Kavin, where are you?"

Kavin's response was laced with fear. "Why, what happened?"

Aarav's words tumbled out in a rush. "Mithra... she's okay, but do you remember the Harsha case?"

Kavin's confusion was evident. "Yes, what about it?"

Aarav's revelation was stunning. "He was murdered by Zoya and Zara."

Kavin's incredulity was palpable. "What? That's impossible. Whoever she kills, she puts paint on them."

Aarav's counterpoint was stark. "But the funds, Kavin. They were transferred to Zara's orphanage."

Kavin's determination kicked in. "I'll inform my team."

Aarav's agreement was swift. "Okay."

As they prepared to end the call, Kavin's voice stopped Aarav. "Aarav, Zoya was dead. Only Zara is alive."

Aarav's shock was evident. "What?"

Kavin's warning was urgent. "Be careful with Rachel."

With that, the call ended, leaving Aarav to process the bombshell revelations. His mind reeled with the implications, his thoughts racing with the danger that lurked in the shadows.

Aarav's words hung in the air, heavy with the weight of revelation. Mithra's eyes widened, her mind struggling to comprehend the truth. Zoya, her friend, was dead. The tears fell like rain, her body trembling with shock.

Aarav's voice cut through the chaos, a stark reminder of the danger that loomed. "Kavin said the police will come here."

Manasvi's concern was immediate. "What about Kavin?"

Aarav's explanation was swift. "He's in Lyziden, but he's on his way to Sisalian now."

Manasvi's arms enveloped Mithra, a comforting embrace that offered little solace. Mithra's mind was a maelstrom of guilt and regret, her thoughts consumed by the what-ifs.

Her voice barely whispered, a haunting refrain. "If I could have been your friend..."

And with that, Mithra's world went dark, her body crumpling to the ground, unconscious. The tears continued to fall, a testament to the anguish that ravaged her soul.

Manasvi's voice was laced with panic, her words a desperate cry. "Mithra, what happened? Mithra!"

Aarav's hands moved swiftly, checking Mithra's pulse with a practiced touch. His face was set in a grim mask, his eyes locked on Mithra's limp form.

Vibha's voice cut through the chaos, her words firm and decisive. "We need to take her to the hospital now!"

Without hesitation, Aarav scooped Mithra into his arms, her body limp and unresponsive. Manasvi and Vibha flanked him, their faces etched with worry, as they rushed towards the door, their hearts racing with fear for Mithra's life.

As they reached the car, Kavin's team entered Harsha's home, their faces set with determination.

Neel and Aarav stepped out of the car, their expressions grim.

Yuan's voice was laced with concern. "What's going on? Where are you guys headed?"

Aarav's explanation was swift. "Sir, Mithra fainted. We're taking her to the hospital."

Kapil's shock was palpable. "What? What happened to her?"

Nithin's calm voice reassured his father. "Dad, we're taking her to the hospital. Neel and Aarav will stay here and keep an eye on things."

Kapil's nod was curt. "Okay, go. Take care of her."

With that, the car sped away, leaving Neel and Aarav to be with them, their minds racing with the implications of Mithra's collapse.

As the team entered Harsha's home, Aarav began to explain the shocking truth. "Harsha's death was no accident. We have evidence that Zoya and Zara were involved in his murder."

He paused, pulling out the document that revealed the fund transfer. "This shows that Harsha's funds were transferred to Zara's orphanage. It's clear that Zara had a motive to kill Harsha."

Neel's eyes widened as he took in the information. "But what about Zoya? Kavin said she was dead."

The team nodded, their faces set with determination. They knew they had to get to the bottom of this complex web of deceit and uncover the truth behind Harsha's tragic death.

Yuan's eyes scanned the room, taking in every detail. His gaze landed on the scribbled papers, and he pointed them. "What's the meaning of these?"

Aarav's expression turned somber. "I think Harsha had multiple personality disorders."

Rahul's curiosity was piqued. "Explain that."

Aarav took a deep breath before launching into an explanation. "Harsha may have taken the wrong drugs, which could have triggered the condition. But there's usually another underlying reason for multiple personalities to emerge."

Smith's eyes narrowed. "What's that reason?"

Aarav's voice was measured. "Severe trauma during early childhood, such as extreme, repetitive physical, sexual, or emotional abuse. This can cause the mind to fragment, creating multiple personalities as a coping mechanism."

The team nodded, their faces reflecting their understanding of the complex psychological dynamics at play. Yuan's eyes, however, remained fixed on the scribbled papers, his mind racing with the implications.

As they pored over the financial records, a chilling discovery emerged. The fund transfer had taken place exactly one week before the fateful day. It was as if the victim had been counting down the days until his demise.

Among the scattered papers, they found a collection of scribbled notes, each one a desperate cry for help. "Sorry, please leave me" was scrawled in hasty handwriting, the words bleeding into one another. Another note read, "I will kill you," the letters sharp and menacing.

But it was the third note that caught Rahul's attention. Tucked away under the bed, it seemed to have been hidden from prying eyes. The message was, "She is in the garden rose."

39

As he gazed at the scribbled words, a shiver ran down Rahul's spine. He felt like he was unraveling a thread that would lead him down a dark and treacherous path. But he couldn't turn back now. The truth was hidden in these cryptic messages, waiting to be unearthed.

Smith's eyes narrowed as he pondered the enigmatic message. "Who is she?" he murmured, his voice barely audible. "And what does 'She is in garden rose' mean?"

Rahul's mind was racing with possibilities. He rapidly searched the room, scouring every inch for a clue. "I think someone has given us a clue," he exclaimed, his eyes locking onto Smith's. "This message is different from the others. It's the only one that's not a threat or a plea for help."

Smith's curiosity was piqued. "How can you be so sure?" he asked, his brow furrowed.

Rahul explained, his words tumbling out in a rush. "He wrote the same sentence on multiple papers, but this one was written only once. And it was hidden under the bed, separated from the others. That's not a coincidence."

Kapil, who had been quietly observing the exchange, nodded in agreement. "You're right, Rahul. This message stands out. Let's get it analyzed by a graphologist. Maybe they can uncover a hidden meaning or identify the writer's handwriting."

Kapil's eyes scanned the room, his gaze lingering on every detail. Suddenly, he stopped in front of a wall that seemed out of place. The paint looked fresh, and the color didn't quite match the surrounding area.

Kapil tapped on the wall, and the sound that echoed back was hollow, unlike the solid thud they expected.

"It sounds like there's a space behind it," Rahul whispered, his eyes wide with excitement.

Smith's eyes narrowed. "A hidden room?"

Kapil nodded, his mind racing. "I think so. Let's find out."

Without hesitation, they started pressing on the wall.

With a collective heave, they pushed the wall, and it finally gave way, crumbling into dust and debris. As the dust settled, they stepped into the hidden room, their eyes adjusting to the darkness.

Rahul fumbled for the light switch, and suddenly, the room was bathed in a warm glow. The space was small, with bare walls and a cold, grey floor. But what caught their attention was a single painting, hanging on the far wall.

Rahul's eyes widened as he gazed at the painting, the words "She is in garden rose" echoing in his mind. The image depicted a young girl standing behind a rose plant in a garden, her finger pointing to the blooming flower. But it was her expression that caught their attention—her face was etched with sadness, and her eyes were brimming with tears.

Smith's voice was barely above a whisper. "She's not just pointing to the rose; she's trying to tell us something."

Kapil's eyes were fixed on the girl's face. "She looks like she's lost something precious."

Rahul's mind was racing. "The rose is the key. But what does it represent?"

As they continued to study the painting.

As they carefully made their way back, they carried the painting, medicine, and scribbled papers with them. The weight of the evidence felt significant, and they knew they had to analyze it further to unravel the mysteries.

"We need to get to the bottom of this," Rahul said, his eyes fixed on the painting.

"And find out who 'she' is," Smith added, his mind still on the enigmatic message.

Kapil nodded, his eyes scanning the papers. "These scribbles might hold more clues. Let's get them to a graphologist ASAP."

As they emerged from the hidden room, they felt a sense of determination. They were one step closer to solving the puzzle, and they wouldn't rest until they uncovered the truth.

With the evidence in hand, they made their way back to their headquarters, ready to dive deeper into the case. The painting, medicine, and scribbled papers held secrets, and they were determined to expose them.

As Kavin stepped into the warm embrace of Mithra's home, he was met with a mix of emotions. Manasvi's gentle smile and welcoming gesture contrasted with the hint of concern in her eyes. "How is she?" Kavin asked, his voice laced with empathy.

Manasvi's response was a subtle nod towards Mithra, who emerged from the shadows of her room. Their eyes met, and

Kavin was struck by the depth of emotion in Mithra's gaze. Sadness, longing, and a hint of desperation swirled together, leaving him breathless.

As Manasvi departed, leaving the two alone, Kavin's concern spilled over. "What happened, Mithra? You seem...lost."

Mithra's voice barely whispered, "I just can't process everything at the same time." Her eyes darted away, avoiding his gaze.

Kavin's heart ached as he reached out, his words gentle. "How do you feel now? Did you take your medicine?"

But Mithra's response was a deflection, her words spilling out in a rush. "Kavin, investigate Harsha's case. I think Zara's involved." The pain in her eyes was palpable, and Kavin's instincts screamed that there was more to the story.

As they prepared to leave for the office, Kavin's concern lingered. "You're not okay, Mithra. Maybe you should take the day off."

But Mithra's determination was unwavering. "Please, I have to go. CB cream is being finalized today."

With a heavy heart, Kavin relented, offering to drive her to the office. As they journeyed together, the silence between them was thick with unspoken emotions, each lost in their own thoughts.

Rahul's eyes remained fixed on the painting, his mind racing with connections. Suddenly, his face lit up with a triumphant smile. "I found it, guys! I found it!" he shouted, his voice echoing through the room.

The others were startled, their faces filled with confusion. "What have you found?" Kapil asked, his brow furrowed.

Rahul's excitement was palpable. "Mr. Kapil, I solved it!" he exclaimed.

Yuan and Smith rushed to his side, curiosity etched on their faces. "What?" they asked in unison.

Rahul took a deep breath, his words tumbling out in a rush. "Look at the painting, the phrase *She is in garden rose*, and the other notes like *Sorry, please leave*. In the painting, the woman is pointing to the rose, and she's sad."

Smith nodded, trying to keep up. "We know that, Rahul."

But Rahul's eyes sparkled with a new revelation. "No, you don't understand. She was buried there."

The room fell silent, the others' faces frozen in shock and confusion. "What buried?" Yuan asked, her voice barely above a whisper.

Rahul's words hung in the air, heavy with implication. The painting, the notes, the mysterious messages—all pointed to a tragic truth. The woman in the painting, the enigmatic "she," was more than just a subject—she was a victim, buried beneath the roses.

As Kavin and Sultan entered, they were met with a mixture of shock and confusion. "What happened? Why do you guys look like you've seen a ghost?" Sultan asked, his curiosity piqued.

Rahul, eager to share his discovery, beckoned them over. "Guys, come here! I've cracked the case!"

As Rahul explained his findings, Smith's eyes widened. "So, we have to dig?"

Rahul nodded nonchalantly. "Yes, we do."

Kavin's expression turned serious. "Guys, we're undercover, and it's not easy to bring in outside help. We're dealing with the Sicilian serial killers, and we only have seven days until November 6th."

Rahul's face fell, his enthusiasm dampened by the reality of their situation.

Just then, Kapil's phone rang, shrill in the tense atmosphere. He answered, and his eyes widened in surprise. "What?...We are coming?" The words hung in the air, confusing everyone.

Kapil's words hung in the air, sparking a flurry of questions. "Why?" Kavin asked, his brow furrowed.

Kapil hesitated before explaining, "A lady has come to the station, claiming she wants to meet the people who went to Harsha's home yesterday."

The team exchanged confused glances, their minds racing with possibilities. Who was this lady? What did she want? And how did she know about their visit to Harsha's home?

40

As they made their way to the police station, the air was thick with unspoken questions. What would they find out? Was this lady connected to the case? And what did she know about the mysterious events unfolding around them?

With each step, the tension grew, their hearts pounding in anticipation. What awaited them at the police station? Only time will tell.

As they entered the police station, a young lady with striking beauty and a fragile demeanor caught their attention. Her eyes were clouded with fear and confusion, and she seemed to be searching for something or someone. The moment she spotted Smith, she rushed towards him with an air of desperation.

"Yesterday, you were the ones who came to Harsha's home," she said, her voice trembling with hope as she gazed up at Smith.

Smith, taken aback by her sudden approach, stepped back and gestured to his team. "We came," he said, indicating that they were all present.

The lady's eyes darted to the others, but her focus remained on Smith. "I want to talk to you," she said, her voice barely above a whisper.

Kavin's curiosity got the best of him. "About what?" he asked, his tone gentle but inquiring.

The lady's expression turned sorrowful, and her eyes seemed to bore into their souls. With a deep breath, she began to speak, her words dripping with emotion. "I'm Lina".

Lina's words poured out like a river, filled with pain and sorrow. "My grandfather and I live in the building opposite Harsha's house. He's the only family I have left. He was a talented painter and always healthy... until Harsha showed up."

She took a deep breath, composing herself. "One day, Harsha and my grandfather met on the street. My grandfather looked terrified. Then, Harsha came to our home when I wasn't there. But I had set up a camera in the hall, and I saw everything."

Lina's eyes welled up with tears as she continued. "Harsha was talking to my grandfather, who looked scared. Then, Harsha took one of my grandfather's paintings from the wall. After Harsha left, I rushed home to find my grandfather's lifeless body. I saw the footage, and it showed Harsha pushing my grandfather before taking the painting."

Lina's voice cracked as she handed the camcorder to the team, her tears flowing uncontrollably. The team watched in silence, their hearts heavy with the weight of her words. The footage revealed a shocking truth, and they knew they had to act swiftly to bring justice to Lina and her grandfather.

Kavin's sentence was cut short as Lina pleaded with him, her eyes brimming with tears. "Sir, I believe you; please do something."

Kavin's expression turned resolute. "Okay, we'll take action. Sultan and Rahul, investigate her claims and check the previous camera records."

He turned to Yuan and Smith, his eyes blazing with intensity. "You two, listen carefully. We've collected information about Zara, who's been hiding behind a mask of Rachel. I want you to dig deeper and uncover her true identity."

Kavin nodded at Kapil, indicating that they had a meeting to attend. The team understood the gravity of the situation and sprang into action, determined to unravel the mysteries surrounding Zara and Harsha.

With a sense of purpose, the team dispersed to tackle their assigned tasks, leaving Kavin and Kapil to head to their meeting, ready to confront the challenges ahead.

Kavin and Kapil entered the IG's office, greeted by a warm welcome.
As they sat down, the IG asked, "What's the latest in the case?

Kavin and Kapil explained the developments, including Zara's revelation and the shocking twist. The IG's expression turned grave upon hearing, "Only seven days left."

The IG's eyes narrowed. "You think Harsha's case is connected to this?"

Kavin nodded. "Yes, sir. We believe he's involved."

The IG's voice turned thoughtful. "They haven't found the body, have they?"

Kavin's expression turned grim. "They have, but they're hiding it. Harsha's challenge to find the body was just a ruse."

The IG's eyes widened in shock. "What are you planning to do?"

Kavin's jaw set in determination. "Sir, I think Advik's father is hiding something to protect his reputation."

The IG's face turned stern. "Don't worry, I'll handle that aspect. You focus on solving the case."

Kavin nodded, relieved. "Thank you, sir." With a sense of determination and renewed purpose, Kavin and Kapil exited the office, ready to tackle the challenges ahead.

As they parted ways, Kavin shared a concern that had been weighing on his mind. "Uncle, I'm heading to the hospital to check on Sunaina's condition. Staying there is becoming increasingly dangerous for her."

Kapil's expression turned solemn, his eyes clouding with a mix of emotions. "Today's a difficult day for me, Kavin. It's my wife's death anniversary."

Kavin's face fell, his voice barely above a whisper. "I'm so sorry, Uncle. I forgot it's also Nithin's birthday."

Kapil's nod was laced with sadness. "Yes, I need to go. I have to pay my respects.

With a gentle nod, Kavin bid his uncle farewell. "Take care, Uncle. Be strong."

As they went their separate ways, the weight of their struggles hung in the air. Kavin's determination to protect Sunaina and unravel the mysteries of the case, and Kapil's poignant journey to confront his past and honor his loved ones.

Kavin trudged through the hospital corridors, his eyes heavy with fatigue, his body weary from the long journey. The overnight trip had taken its toll, but his determination to see Sunaina and ensure her safety propelled him forward.

As he approached her ward, he took a deep breath, stealing himself for what lay ahead. He pushed open the door, his gaze scanning the room until it landed on Sunaina's fragile form, lying still in the bed.

Kavin emerged from Sunaina's ward, not wanting to disturb her peaceful slumber. His next stop was the neurologist's office, seeking answers about her recovery. He knocked on the door, and the head of neurology welcomed him with a warm smile.

As Kavin took a seat, he asked the question that had been weighing on his mind. "Doctor, how is she? Can we discharge her soon?"

The neurologist's expression turned cautious. "She needs at least a week to recover. She's experiencing sudden head pains, and we need to continue her treatment."

Kavin's eyes widened in shock. "Is there another problem, Doctor?"

The neurologist reassured him, "Don't worry, she'll recover soon. We're providing advanced treatment and medication."

Kavin's concern lingered, and he asked, "Can we shift her to a safer location?"

The doctor's expression turned grave. "No, that would be more dangerous for her."

Kavin's confusion deepened. "What can we do, then?"

The neurologist's advice was clear. "Keep the police out of her ward. We can't risk any further complications."

With a sense of tension and uncertainty, Kavin left the office, his mind racing with thoughts and concerns.

As Kavin entered Aarav's cabin, he was greeted with a warm smile. "Hi, Kavin! How are you?" Aarav's enthusiasm was palpable; he was happy to see his friend after a long time.

Kavin forced a nod, trying to appear calm despite the turmoil brewing inside. "Fine," he replied, downplaying the stress of the case.

Aarav gestured to the couch, inviting Kavin to sit. "Come, sit down." As they settled in, Aarav's eyes sparkled with curiosity. "So, what brings you here today? You look like you've got a lot on your mind."

"I want Harsha's autopsy report and his girlfriend's number," Kavin came to the point.

"Oh, sorry, I forgot." Aarav got up to take the report, and he handed it over to him.

"Thank you. As Kavin stood up to leave, his exhaustion caught up with him, and he felt a wave of dizziness wash over him. He stumbled and sat back down on the couch, his vision blurring.

Aarav's concern was immediate. "What's wrong, Kavin? You look like you're about to pass out."

Kavin rubbed his eyes, trying to shake off the fatigue. "I didn't sleep last night. I drove all night to get here."

Aarav's expression turned stern. "Kavin, you need to take care of yourself. Go get some sleep before you start working on the case again."

Kavin nodded reluctantly, knowing Aarav was right. "Okay, bye."

As he reached the door, Aarav called out, "Bye, take care! You came alone, didn't you?"

Kavin nodded, his voice barely above a whisper. "Yes."

Aarav's warning followed him out the door. "Don't drive; it's not safe. Get a cab."

But Kavin ignored the advice, his determination to solve the case overriding his concern for his well-being. He got behind the wheel and drove from the hospital to their place, his eyelids heavy with fatigue, his mind racing with thoughts of the case.

41

As the darkness outside signaled the end of the day, Kavin's teammates began to trickle in, exhausted from their respective tasks. But Kavin, who had caught a few hours of sleep, was already up and about, having ordered dinner for everyone.

As they gathered around the table, Rahul expressed his gratitude. "Thanks, Kavin, you ordered food. We're starving!

But Yuan's expression was tense, his eyes clouded with concern. "Kavin, Zara has absconded.

Kavin's response was calm and assured. "She's just hiding. She'll come to Sunaina eventually."

Sultan, who had been quiet until now, spoke up, his voice laced with fatigue. "Let's eat first. I'm too tired to think straight."

The team nodded in agreement, digging into the food as they shared stories of their day. But beneath the surface, tension simmered, fueled by the knowledge that Zara was still out there, and Sunaina's safety hung in the balance.

The room fell silent as the Sultan's words hung in the air. "Someone is helping Zara."

Kavin's eyes widened in shock, his mind racing with the implications. "What? That's impossible!"

Yuan's expression turned grave. "We don't know where she was hiding. We can't rule out the possibility of an accomplice.

As they finished dinner, Rahul spoke up, his voice measured. "We investigated Riya, Harsha's girlfriend. She seemed innocent, but I have some doubts about the girl we met today."

Smith's eyes lit up, his voice filled with excitement. "Lina?"

All eyes turned to him, surprised by his sudden interjection.

Smith's face turned bright red as he trailed off, his shyness getting the better of him. The team's attention shifted back to Rahul, who continued his report.

"I think Lina is innocent, but one thing is clear: Harsha has a secret, and it's hidden in the garden behind a rose. And I believe it's a dead body."

Rahul's words hung in the air, leaving the team stunned and confused. But he wasn't finished yet.

"There's one more thing. We have a lead on a person who frequently crosses Harsha's house and works at the cafe where Harsha usually buys coffee."

Rahul pulled out his phone and showed them a photo of a young man with a familiar face. The team's eyes widened as they recognized the boy from the cafe.

"Who is he?" Kavin asked, his curiosity piqued.

Rahul's expression turned serious. "His name is Dhruv. And I think he might be the key to unlocking Harsha's secrets."

Rahul's revelation left the team stunned. "He worked there for only one week and resigned on the exact day of Harsha's death."

Before Rahul could continue, Yuan's eyes widened in surprise. "I know him!

Kavin's curiosity was piqued. "You know him?"

Yuan's memory flashed back to the cake shop incident. "He's the boy from the cake shop, the one Yamini shouted at when we were getting a birthday cake for her mother."

Smith's eyes lit up. "Yes, that's him!"

Rahul nodded. "We've seen him in the CCTV footage, but I didn't think much of him until now."

Determined to investigate further, Rahul declared, "I have to go to the cake shop."

Sultan offered to join him, but Rahul insisted he rest. However, Sultan was adamant, "Kavin only drove the car, I had a good sleep."

Smith intervened, "Sultan, you stay; I'll go with him."

Kavin agreed, "Yes, that's right."

With a plan in place, Rahul and Smith set off towards the cake shop, leaving the others to ponder the new developments.

Rahul and Smith entered the cake shop, approaching the cashier at the counter. Rahul flashed his ID card and showed the photo of Rohan. "Do you know him?"

The cashier's eyes widened in recognition. "Yes, Dhruv worked here."

Rahul pressed on. "Where is he now?"

The cashier replied, "He resigned two weeks ago."

Smith's eyes narrowed. "Why did he resign?"

The cashier hesitated before answering, "He said his mother was sick, and he needed to take care of her."

Rahul asked, "What was his shift timing?"

The cashier responded, "Evening shift, sir."

Smith inquired, "Did you find him suspicious at all?"

The cashier shook his head. "No, he was kind to the staff and customers."

Rahul handed over his contact information. "If you see him anywhere, please call me."

As they turned to leave, the cashier asked, his voice laced with curiosity, "Sir, why are you asking about him?"

Rahul and Smith just smiled and left the shop, leaving the cashier with unanswered questions.

Yuan's voice was laced with a mix of frustration and disappointment as he conveyed the news to Kavin. "I went to search for Zara at school, but she was nowhere to be found. The details we had were fake, Kavin. It was a dead end."

೧

Kavin's expression turned grim, his mind racing with the implications. "What?" he pressed, his tone firm but laced with a hint of concern.

As Rahul and Smith returned to their meeting point, they found Kavin waiting for them, his expression expectant. But upon seeing their somber faces, his expression turned concerned. "What happened?"

Rahul shook his head, disappointment etched on his face. "He resigned two weeks ago."

Kavin's eyes narrowed, his mind racing with the implications. "Okay, what's the plan now?"

Rahul with confusion "I have to think."

Yuan can't find Zara and the school she was working at. The days are passing; they are reaching the day they marked. They investigate people and search in places.

Kapil's eyes scanned the room, his voice steady as he revealed the latest breakthrough. "Rahul, the graphologist's report is in. It seems we have a twist."

Rahul's curiosity was piqued, his eyes locked onto Kapil.

"The threatening note, 'I will kill you,' was written by one person," Kapil began. "But the apologetic message, 'Sorry, please leave me,' and the poem, 'She is in the garden, rose,' were written by another."

Rahul's eyes widened, his mind racing with the implications.

"And?" he prompted, his voice barely above a whisper.

Kapil's expression turned grim. "The second person, the one who wrote the poem and the apology, was Harsha."

Rahul's eyes snapped to the report in Kapil's hand, his mind reeling with the revelation. The case had just taken a dramatic turn, and the truth was finally beginning to unravel.

Rahul's determination was evident. "I want to know what's under the rose."

Kavin nodded, his mind already working on the next step. "Tomorrow, you go and check. I'll arrange for people to be there."

Rahul's face lit up with a hint of a smile, relieved that the investigation was moving forward. "Okay."

With a plan in place, the trio retired for the night, their minds still racing with questions and theories but determined to uncover the truth.

Kapil's voice echoed through the room, waking up the sleeping team members. "Kavin, Yuan, Rahul, come out!"

As they gathered around, Rahul asked, "What happened, Uncle?"

Sultan raised an eyebrow. "Uncle?"

Yuan chuckled, "They became close."

Rahul warmly hugged Kapil. "How are you?"

Kapil smiled, "Fine, fine. I brought breakfast."

After freshening up, they sat down to enjoy the meal Kapil had brought. As they ate, Kapil informed Rahul, "I arranged for people to come to Harsha's home. You can start your work."

Smith asked, "Do you think there's a dead body?"

Rahul's expression turned serious. "Yes, I do."

With their plan in place, the team finished their breakfast, prepared themselves, and headed out to start their investigation at Harsha's home.

Yuan announced, "I'm going to Zoya's school where you all study."

Smith nodded, accepting his role. "Okay, I'll come with you."

As they prepared to leave, they reviewed their questions and plan, ensuring they were ready for the investigation. Yuan and Smith aimed to uncover more about Zara's activities and potential involvement in Harsha's disappearance.

"I think we will find Zara there," Yuan said.

With their strategy in place, Yuan and Smith set off towards the school, determined to gather more information and piece together the puzzle.

42

Rahul and the team arrived at Harsha's home, their hearts racing with anticipation and a hint of trepidation. They had been preparing for this moment for what felt like an eternity.

The girl's painting had provided a crucial clue, pointing to a specific spot in the garden where they believed they would find the truth.

With shovels in hand, they began digging at the designated spot, their movements methodical and deliberate. The sound of dirt and gravel filled the air as they carefully excavated the earth.

As the team dug deeper, a putrid smell wafted through the air, forcing them to cover their noses with masks. The stench grew stronger, and their hearts sank with a sense of foreboding.

Finally, their shovels hit something solid. With trembling hands, they carefully uncovered the truth. A lifeless body lay before them, its presence both shocking and devastating.

The team stood in stunned silence, their minds struggling to process the gruesome discovery. The news spread like wildfire, drawing the press and media channels to the scene.

Reporters swarmed the area, cameras flashing and microphones thrust forward. "Breaking news: Police have found a dead body!" The headlines screamed.

Rahul's team stood amidst the chaos, their faces etched with a mix of emotions—shock, sadness, and a hint of relief that the truth was finally out.

The team accompanied the body to the hospital, surrounded by a swarm of reporters firing off questions.

"Is this a female or male body?"

"What happening?"

"Who committed this murder?"

"Is this the work of a serial killer?"

"Have you identified the killer?"

"Sir, can you tell us what's happening?"

The reporters' voices grew louder and more insistent, but Rahul and the team remained tight-lipped, refusing to comment. They pushed through the crowd, their faces stern, and entered the hospital, leaving the chaos behind. The medical team took charge of the body, and the investigation continued, but the team's silence only fueled the media frenzy.

The doctors finally emerged with the autopsy report, their faces somber. "It was a female body, aged between 21 and 25," they announced, handing Kavin and Rahul the report. As they opened the folder, they saw a phone, chain, and ring neatly arranged on the cover page. The personal belongings of the victim.

"We can know who is with the help of the phone," Rahul says.

Sultan nodded and said, "I'll try to recover the data. Maybe we can find some clues about her identity and who might have been in contact with her."

Sultan left with the phone, determined to unlock its secrets.

Meanwhile, Rahul turned to Kapil and asked, "Mr. Kapil, can you check the missing persons cases from the past two months? Maybe we can find a match."

Kapil nodded and headed out to start his search.

As the team dispersed to tackle their tasks, the investigation continued to unfold, each step bringing them closer to unraveling the mystery of the unknown dead body.

Yuan and Smith arrived at Zara's school and made their way to the principal's office. They were greeted by a middle-aged woman with a kind face, who introduced herself as Principal Mrs. Kumar.

Principal Kumar sat serenely in her cabin, exuding an air of quiet authority. Her raven tresses were neatly coiled into a bun, flecked with wisps of silver that betrayed her years of experience. Behind her glasses, her eyes sparkled with a sharp intelligence, missing nothing.

She pored over the papers scattered before her, her brow furrowed in concentration. In her hand, a pen spun lazily, a habitual gesture that revealed her introspective nature.

The soft glow of the desk lamp cast a warm light on her composed features, creating an atmosphere of studious calm. Yet, as Yuan and Smith approached, a flicker of curiosity danced across her face, hinting at a depth of emotion beneath her tranquil surface.

Yuan and Smith exchanged a knowing glance as they sat down in the principal's cabin. They flashed their ID cards, and Principal Kumar's expression turned attentive.

"We're police officers, ma'am," Yuan explained. "We're investigating a case and need information about someone."

The principal nodded, her eyes sparkling with curiosity. "How may I help you?"

Smith showed her the photo of Zara. "Do you know her?"

Principal Kumar's face lit up with recognition. "That's Teacher Rachel. She was one of our math teachers."

Yuan's eyes narrowed. "Where is she now?"

"She resigned two weeks ago," the principal replied.

Yuan's brow furrowed. "Resigned? Why?"

"Her mother was sick, and she wanted to take care of her," Principal Kumar explained.

Smith's eyes locked onto the principal. "But she has no parents."

The principal's expression faltered, and she shifted uncomfortably in her seat.

Yuan's voice was firm. "Do you have her resume?"

The principal hesitated before searching for the document. Finally, she handed over the resume.

Yuan scanned it before showing the principal a photo of Dhuruv from the cake shop. "Do you see him with Rachel?"

The principal's eyes widened. "Not Rachel; he's Dhuruv, the boyfriend of Teacher Kiran."

Smith's eyes snapped with interest. "Kiran? Who is she?"

"Our school math teacher," the principal replied.

Yuan's gaze was intense. "Do you have her photo?"

The principal nodded and flipped through a magazine on her desk, stopping at a page with a familiar face. "This is Kiran."

Yuan's eyes locked onto the principal. "Can you call Kiran here?"

The principal's expression turned guarded, hinting at a secret. "You don't know..."

Yuan's curiosity was piqued. "What do we not know?"

The principal hesitated before speaking. "She hasn't been coming to school for two to three months."

Smith's brow furrowed. "Why?"

The principal's voice was laced with uncertainty. "We don't know. I asked Rachel if she was close to Kiran, and she said Kiran went to her native place to convince her parents to allow her to marry Dhuruv."

Yuan's mind was racing. "Can you give us Kiran's photo?"

The principal nodded, handing over the resume. "But please, don't take this with you."

Smith took a photo of the resume and handed it back to the principal. "Okay, ma'am. Thank you."

Yuan and Smith left the cabin, armed with photos of Kiran and Zara's resumes, their minds buzzing with new information and unanswered questions. The investigation had just taken an intriguing turn.

43

Mithra sat at her desk, her eyes fixed on the news report on her computer screen. The headline read: "Dead Body Found at Harsha's Residence.". She felt a shiver run down her spine as she read the details of the discovery.

Mithra's hands trembled as she dialed Manasvi's number. "Hello, Mithra," Manasvi answered, her voice calm and reassuring.

"Manasvi, did you know whose body it is?" Mithra asked, her voice laced with fear and confusion.

"I don't know, and we didn't telecast any information about the identity of the body," Manasvi replied, trying to calm Mithra down.

Mithra's mind was racing. "Is it Zoya's dead body?" she asked, her thoughts filled with worst-case scenarios.

"Mithra, please be calm," Manasvi tried to console her. "We'll find out soon."

But Mithra was insistent. "Please, I want to know," she begged.

"Okay, I'll call Kavin and find out," Manasvi promised, trying to reassure her.

The two friends ended the call, leaving Mithra in a state of anxious suspense, her heart racing with anticipation and fear.

Kavin's phone rang, breaking the silence. "Hello, Kavin. What's happening?" Manasvi asked, her voice laced with confusion.

"How did the media find out about this?" Kavin asked, his tone firm and investigative.

"Someone from the public called and informed us," Manasvi replied, her voice defensive.

Kavin's grip on the phone tightened. "The public? How did they know?"

Manasvi sighed. "I don't know, Kavin. My dean was pressuring us to report on it, but I didn't reveal anything. I'm waiting for your confirmation."

Kavin's voice was resolute. "I'll inform you after we catch the killer."

Manasvi's tone was urgent. "Please, make it fast. The media is breathing down my neck."

The call ended, leaving Kavin to focus on the investigation while Manasvi was left to navigate the pressure from her dean and the media.

Kavin's phone rang again, and he answered, "Hello, Uncle."

"Kavin, I searched, but there's no missing case matching the victim's description," Kapil informed, his voice firm and matter-of-fact.

Kavin's expression turned thoughtful. "Okay, Uncle. Thanks for checking."

The conversation was brief, and they ended the call. Kavin's mind was already racing with the implications.

No missing person's report meant the victim might not have been reported missing.

Smith's eyes were fixed on the news report as he turned to Yuan. "We have to go there," he said, his voice firm and urgent.

Yuan nodded in agreement. "We have to; let's go to the hospital."

As they rushed to the hospital, Smith quickly dialed Rahul's number. "Rahul, where are you?" he asked, his voice firm and commanding.

"I'm at Sisalian General Hospital; come fast," Rahul replied, his voice laced with a sense of gravity.

Smith and Yuan ended the call and quickly emerged at the hospital, their hearts racing with anticipation and concern. They knew that every minute counted, and they had to get to the bottom of the mystery.

As they entered the hospital, they were met with a sense of chaos and urgency. Doctors and nurses rushed past them, their faces filled with concern. Smith and Yuan knew they had to find Rahul and get an update on the situation. They quickly scanned the area, their eyes locking onto Rahul's familiar figure in the distance.

"Rahul!" Smith shouted, his voice echoing through the hospital corridor.

Rahul turned, his expression grim. "Smith, I told you there could be a dead body," he said, his voice low and serious.

Smith's eyes narrowed. "Did you guys find out who she is?"

Rahul shook his head. "No, we found a phone on her, but Sultan's working on recovering the data."

Smith's gaze intensified. "What does the autopsy say? How did she die?"

Rahul's face turned somber. "She's been tortured, and the cause of death is a severe head injury from an iron rod."

Smith and Yuan were shocked, their eyes widening in horror. The brutality of the crime scene was beyond anything they had imagined. They stood there for a moment, processing the gruesome details, their minds racing with questions and suspicions.

Kavin walked in, looking concerned, and Yuan immediately asked him, "Kavin, what happened? How does the media know about this?"

Kavin explained, "Manasvi said someone from the public called them."

Yuan's eyes narrowed. "Who is she?"

Kavin shook his head. "I asked Kapil to check the missing cases, but he just called and said there's no match."

Kavin's expression turned thoughtful. "What about the Zara case?"

Yuan's eyes widened. "One new person has entered both Harsha and Zara's cases."

Kavin's voice was laced with shock. "Who?"

Yuan revealed, "Dhruv's girlfriend, Kiran."

Smith showed them Kiran's photo, and Rahul's eyes widened in disbelief. He rummaged through the dead body's belongings and pulled out a chain with a small red stone pendant, identical to the one in the photo.

The group stared at each other in shock, their eyes fixed on the chain. The revelation was unbelievable, and they struggled to process the connection between Kiran and the dead body.

"Guys!" Sultan called out, breaking the stunned silence. They turned to see him running towards them, out of breath.

"I recorded all the data, luckily, and here are her photos," Sultan explained, handing them a pen drive. "I transferred all the data into this pen drive."

Yuan took the pen drive and inserted it into his phone. As he scrolled through the data, his eyes widened in shock, and he became speechless.

Yuan showed the contents to the others, and Sultan's eyes landed on Smith's phone, displaying Kiran's picture.

"How did you get this picture?" Sultan asked, confusion etched on his face.

Kavin's voice was laced with realization. "So, Kiran was dead, and she was Dhruv's girlfriend."

The group stood there, trying to process the shocking revelation. The pen drive's contents had uncovered a web of secrets, and they were determined to unravel the mystery.

44

"Sir, someone took the dead body! Catch him!" a doctor shouted, alerting the team to the unfolding situation.

The team sprang into action, rushing from the ground floor to the parking lot. They were met with a shocking sight: the person was already putting the body into a car.

Despite their swift response, they were too late. The person sped away, leaving the team to chase. They quickly jumped into their vehicles and began a high-stakes pursuit, determined to catch the culprit and recover the stolen body.

The person was wearing a black hoodie and had their face covered with a black mask, making it impossible to identify them. They were trying to remain anonymous and escape detection, but the team was hot on their heels.

As they sped through the streets, the person's car swerved and turned, trying to shake off the pursuers. But the team was relentless, staying close behind and refusing to give up.

The person's identity remained a mystery, but their actions were becoming increasingly desperate. The chase continued, with the team determined to uncover the truth and bring the perpetrator to justice.

The car chase reached its climax as the team finally cornered the mysterious figure. With precision and skill, they boxed in the vehicle from all sides, leaving no room for escape. The black hoodie and mask seemed to shimmer in the sunlight as the driver realized the game was up. The team held their breath as they approached the car, ready to uncover the secrets that had been hidden for so long.

As they approached the car with guns drawn, their voices were firm and commanding.

"Get down! Hands up!" they shouted in unison, the words echoing through the stillness like a death knell.

The man, realizing the futility of resistance, slowly raised his hands in surrender, his eyes fixed on the barrel of the gun trained on him. With a sense of resignation, he slid out of the car, his movements deliberate and calculated.

As he stood there, exposed and vulnerable, the team closed in, their guns still trained on him. One of them approached the car, peering inside to confirm their worst suspicions. The body, pale and lifeless, lay slumped in the passenger seat, a grim testament to the man's guilt.

They took off his mask; he was Dhuruv Kiran's boyfriend.

With a swift motion, the team handcuffed him, the metal clicking into place with a sense of finality. "You're under arrest," they intoned, the words a solemn ritual marking the end of one journey and the beginning of another.

As they led him away, the man's eyes darted back to the car, his gaze lingering on the body, a mixture of emotions playing across his face. Regret, sorrow, and a hint of defiance all swirled together, a complex dance of feelings that would only begin to unravel in the days to come.

As they dragged the mysterious figure away, he caught sight of the dead body being taken to the hospital and let out a primal scream. "Don't dare to touch her!" he yelled, his eyes wild with a mix of fear and desperation.

But his pleas fell on deaf ears. Smith gave him a sharp pinch, and the team dragged him to their car, throwing him into the back seat. They sped away to their investigation site, a nondescript building on the outskirts of town.

Once inside, the team began their interrogation. Smith's punch sent blood flying from the man's mouth as he slumped in his chair. "Who are you?" Smith demanded. "What's your connection to the victim?"

The man spat out blood, his eyes darting around the room in search of an escape. But there was none. He was trapped, and the team would stop at nothing to uncover the truth.

The interrogation room was thick with tension as Kavin's questions pierced the air. "Why did you try to steal her body?" he asked, his eyes narrowing.

Dhruv's laughter was laced with sarcasm. "Stole? She's, my girl. If anyone tries to hurt her, I'll kill them." His voice trembled with emotion.

Kavin's gaze bore into him. "So, you killed Harsha, right?"

Dhruv's eyes flashed with anger, but he nodded, his voice barely above a whisper. "Yes."

The team exchanged somber glances. Kavin pressed on. "Why did you kill Harsha?"

Dhruv's tears flowed freely now. "I'll kill anyone who influences school students to take drugs. And he was the one who murdered my girlfriend brutally." His words hung in the air like a challenge.

Kavin's expression remained unyielding. "So, you killed him. You should have filed a complaint."

Dhruv's gaze turned icy. "Did anyone file a complaint against me or for Harsha? Then how are you involved?"

Kavin's voice softened slightly. "Why did he kill your girlfriend?"

Dhruv's body shuddered as he recounted the events. "She discovered one of her students was taking drugs, and Harsha was the supplier. She went to his home to warn him, but he tortured her...and killed her with an iron rod." Dhruv's sobs echoed through the room. "She could have called out for me, trusted me, hoped for me...but I wasn't there. Now I've lost her."

The team's faces reflected their empathy, moved by Dhruv's anguish and the depth of his feelings for his lost love.

Kavin's question hung in the air, a gentle probe into the depths of Dhruv's pain. "Kiran's parents know about this?"

Dhruv's voice cracked, his words laced with anguish. "How? How can I tell them that she's gone? That the killer hid her body like she meant nothing?" His volume rose, a mixture of frustration and despair.

The team's expressions remained somber, their eyes filled with compassion. They knew that Dhruv's torment was only beginning, that the weight of his secrets and his loss would haunt him for a long time to come.

Dhruv's eyes seemed to glaze over, lost in the memories of a lifetime. "Do you know how many years we were in a relationship?" he asked, his voice barely above a whisper.

He paused, collecting his thoughts. "From childhood...since I was 3 years old, she has been with me. We grew up together, explored the world together...and for two months, she was trapped in the sinful land of Harsha."

The team exchanged somber glances, the weight of Dhruv's words settling in. A lifetime of love, of memories, of shared experiences...all torn apart by the brutal hand of fate.

Kavin's eyes narrowed, his voice firm. "What happened? How do you know?"

Dhruv's jaw clenched, his words barely above a whisper. "I saw him buried."

Kavin's gaze intensified. "You saw how?

Dhruv's tension was palpable. "I told you, I saw."

Kavin's eyes seemed to bore into Dhruv's soul. "Whom are you trying to save?"

Dhruv's voice was laced with defiance. "No one."

But Kavin's next question caught him off guard. "Zara? You're trying to save Zara?"

Dhruv's eyes widened, his words faltering. "Zara? Why are you involved in her?"

Kavin's grip on Dhruv's arm tightened. "Where is Zara?"

Dhruv's gaze dropped, his voice barely audible. "I don't know."

Kavin's eyes flashed with anger. "She helped you kill Harsha?"

Dhruv's response was swift, his words laced with protectiveness. "No, I killed him."

Kavin's eyes narrowed. "What's your plan?"

Dhruv's smile was laced with sarcasm. "The day after tomorrow, Sunaina will die."

Kavin's grip on Dhruv's collar tightened. "How? Tell me!"

Dhruv's eyes seemed to glint with a challenge. "If you can save the last one, save her.

Kavin's voice was low and menacing. "Who is the last one?"

Dhruv's smile grew wider, his eyes glinting with a mix of emotions. "Find it."

45

As the heavy prison doors closed behind Dhruv, Kavin and the team couldn't shake off the feeling of unease. Their minds raced with thoughts and plans, all centered around saving Sunaina. Kavin's instructions were swift and decisive, his team nodding in unison.

"Mr. Kapil, make the police force surround Sunaina's hospital. I want every update and check with the doctors treating her. Collect details of the doctors," Kavin ordered.

"Stop Yuan, where you'll find Zara in Zoya school. Then she must be hiding in Zoya's house," Kavin continued, his eyes locked on Yuan.

Yuan's voice was laced with confusion. "We have to go to Lyziden?"

Kavin shook his head. "No, in Sisalian, there's an old house of Zoya's. That's our destination."

With a nod, Kapil and Sultan rushed off to set up the police force at the hospital, while Kavin, Smith, Yuan, and Rahul sped towards Zoya's house, their hearts racing with anticipation. As they approached the old house, a sense of foreboding settled over them.

As they entered Zoya's house, an eerie silence enveloped them, punctuated only by the soft creaking of old wooden floorboards beneath their feet. A thick layer of dust coated every surface, giving the impression that the house had been abandoned for years. The team fanned out, searching every room, their guns drawn, ready for a potential confrontation. Kavin's voice boomed through the hallway, echoing off the walls.

"Zara, where are you hiding? We have the order to shoot you. Don't play smart; the game is over!"

But their search yielded nothing. No sign of Zara, no hint of her presence. As they regrouped outside, frustration etched on their faces, the darkness seemed to close in around them.

"Where is she hiding?" Yuan exclaimed, his voice laced with exasperation.

As they turned to leave, Rahul's sharp eyes caught sight of something they had missed earlier—a small entrance to a basement, almost invisible beside the house.

"Wait!" Rahul exclaimed, his voice low and urgent. "There's a basement here."

The team rushed towards it, their hearts racing with anticipation. As they descended into the darkness. This was the same basement where Zara had held Yamini captive.

Their phone torches cast flickering shadows on the walls as they made their way deeper into the basement. The air was thick with dust and the stench of decay. Finally, they reached a small table, and on it, a handwritten note. Kavin's eyes scanned the page, his expression grim.

"What does it say?" Yuan asked, his voice barely above a whisper.

The note ended with a chilling promise:

The game was not over.

I will finish it soon.

-Zara.

Kavin's eyes narrowed, his mind racing with the implications. Zara was always one step ahead, anticipating their every move. The basement, once a potential lead, was now a haunting reminder of their failure to outsmart her.

The team's search yielded nothing but dust and shadows. The basement was empty, devoid of any clues or hints. It was as if Zara had vanished into thin air, leaving behind only her ominous message.

With a sense of urgency, they left the basement and headed to the hospital, their hearts heavy with the knowledge that time was running out for Sunaina. The game was far from over, and Zara's next move was still unknown.

Kavin's phone rang, breaking the tension. He answered, and Manasvi's voice was on the other end.
"Kavin, what happened? Did you find the killer?"

Kavin took a deep breath and explained everything—the twists and turns of the case, Dhruv's confession, and Zara's ominous message. Manasvi listened intently, her silence a testament to her focus.

When Kavin finished, Manasvi asked, "Okay, what do I have to do now?"

Kavin's voice was firm, his confidence unwavering. "Telecast the news of the Harsha case. Tell them we will find the serial killer."

Manasvi's response was crisp. "Okay, Kavin. Tomorrow, sharp at 7:00, the news will be out."

With that, they ended their conversation. Kavin felt a sense of determination wash over him.

The team stood vigilant outside Sunaina's ward, their eyes scanning every nook and cranny with an intensity that rivaled an eagle's gaze. Each member was acutely aware of their surroundings, their senses heightened as they watched for any sign of Zara or her accomplices. Kavin's eyes narrowed, his gaze sweeping the area with a precision that missed nothing. Yuan's head swiveled, his eyes darting between the nurses' station and the patient rooms. Smith's arms were crossed, his eyes fixed on the ward entrance, ready to pounce at a moment's notice. Rahul's eyes scanned the windows, his mind racing with scenarios.

Together, they formed a formidable team, united in their determination to protect Sunaina and bring Zara to justice. Their sharp eyes missed nothing, their focus laser-like as they waited for any sign of movement. The tension was palpable, the air thick with anticipation. They were ready for whatever came next.

The night passed without incident, and the team breathed a collective sigh of relief as the sun rose on a new day. But they knew that the calm was deceptive, and the next 24 hours would be crucial.

As the clock struck 7:00 AM, the news channels sprang to life, and Manasvi's voice rang out clear and confident.

Manasvi's voice was clear and confident as she delivered the breaking news on WAN-K NEWS. The camera zoomed in on her face, her expression serious and professional.

Hello and welcome to WAN-K NEWS. I'm Manasvi.

We have shocking news for you today.

Yesterday, police found a female dead body in the garden of Harsha's home.

Harsha, a notorious drug supplier, had been influencing school students to take drugs.

The victim, a brave teacher, had discovered Harsha's secret and warned him, but he brutally murdered her.

He torched her and killed her with an iron rod on the head; it was the cause of death.

She was Kiran's mathematics teacher in Sisalian matriculation and higher secondary school.

Kiran's boyfriend came to about her death.

So, he planned to murder as he torched his girlfriend.

He used several drugs that pushed him to hallucinate and have multiple disorders.

The police have arrested Dhruv and handed him over to the court.

Manasvi's expression turned grim.

"But that's not the end. The police have promised to arrest the serial killer terrorizing Sicilian. And we have just received word that they have reached the killer. We will provide more information as soon as we get it.

The camera zoomed out as Manasvi concluded, "Thank you for your time. We will keep you updated on this developing story."

The news telecast ended, but the impact lingered. The people of Sisalian were on edge, waiting for the next update, hoping for justice to be served. The police were closing in on the serial killer, and the city held its breath.

Kavin's phone rang, breaking his concentration. He answered, and Mithra's voice was on the other end. "Mithra, how are you?" he asked, trying to sound calm.

"I'm okay; I have news for you," Mithra replied, her voice excited.

"What is it?" Kavin asked, his curiosity piqued.

"Tomorrow, my CB cream is going to launch," Mithra announced.

Kavin's eyes widened in surprise. "What? Tomorrow?"

Mithra laughed. "Yes, I know you're busy, but I wanted to inform you first. Tomorrow is a big day for me."

Kavin's mind was still reeling from the news. "Okay, congrats," he managed to say, still distracted by the case.

Mithra's voice turned serious. "Bye, take care of yourself."

Kavin suddenly remembered his priority. "Mithra, be careful. Inform me if you see Zara anywhere."

With that, they ended the call. Kavin's eyes narrowed, his mind racing with possibilities.

46

Kavin, Smith, and Rahul stood outside the courtroom, their faces set with determination. Today was the day Dhruv would face justice for his actions. As they entered the courtroom, the air was thick with tension.

Dhruv was already seated, his eyes fixed on the floor. Kavin's gaze met him, and for a moment, they just stared at each other. Dhruv's eyes seemed to hold a mix of emotions—guilt, regret, and a hint of defiance.

The judge entered, and the room fell silent. "This court is now in session," the judge declared, his voice commanding attention.

Kavin, Smith, and Rahul took their seats, their eyes fixed on the proceedings. The prosecutor began, outlining the case against Dhruv. Dhruv's lawyer argued for leniency, citing mitigating circumstances.

As the arguments concluded, the judge deliberated, his face stern. Finally, he spoke, "Dhruv, you have been found guilty of manslaughter. Your actions, though driven by a desire for revenge, were unjustifiable. I hereby sentence you to six years in prison."

The courtroom erupted into a flurry of activity as Dhruv was led away. Kavin, Smith, and Rahul exchanged somber glances.

As the sun dipped below the horizon, casting a golden glow over the hospital, the team's nerves began to fray. The day's events had been a rollercoaster, with Dhruv's sentencing leaving a sense of unease.

Now, as night descended, the tension mounted. Zara's next move weighed heavily on their minds. Would she strike again or lay low?

Dr. Sunil made his rounds, checking on Sunaina's progress. Her vitals were stable, but the team knew better than to let their guard down.

Outside the ward, the police presence was a reassuring sight. Officers stood watch, their eyes scanning the corridors for any sign of suspicious activity.

The team stood vigilant, their eyes locked onto the ward entrance. They scrutinized every face, every movement, their senses on high alert.

As the clock struck midnight, the date rolled over to November 6. The team exchanged uneasy glances. Would this day bring more danger, more uncertainty?

Dr. Sunil's calm demeanor masked the turmoil brewing inside. As he entered his cabin, the sound of a gunshot shattered the silence. The team's eyes widened in horror as they rushed towards the source of the noise.

Inside the cabin, they found Dr. Sunil slumping over his desk, a gun lying nearby. The police swiftly took control, securing the area and beginning their investigation.

As Kavin and the team entered Sunaina's ward, they were met with a sight that made their blood run cold. Yellow paint covered the floor, and a line on the ventilator screen seemed to mock them. Rahul's voice was barely above a whisper, "She's dead."

Suntan's eyes blazed with anger. "Sunil did this."

But Smith's expression was skeptical. "Then why did he kill himself?"

Rahul's gaze fell on Sunaina's face. "Her cheek was torn."

Yuan's question hung in the air, "What do we have to do now?"

As they exited the ward, a nurse approached Kavin, out of breath. "Sir, someone wants to talk to you."

Kavin took the phone, his mind racing with thoughts of who it could be. But nothing could have prepared him for the sight on the screen. The phone number widened his eyes in shock.

Kavin's voice trembled as he spoke, "Hello, Mithra?" But the response sent chills down his spine.

"Zara," the voice said, dripping with malice.

Kavin's face contorted in fear, "Zara! Where is Mithra? What have you done to her?" he demanded, his voice laced with tension and nervousness.

Zara's laughter was like ice picks to Kavin's soul, "She's the last one."

Kavin's eyes widened, his mind racing with worst-case scenarios. "Don't dare to touch her!" he shouted, his voice echoing through the hospital corridor.

Zara's sarcasm cut deep: "I let her launch her dream project, and now it's my dream time."

Kavin's grip on the phone tightened, his knuckles white with rage and fear. He knew Zara's games, her twisted mind. Mithra was in grave danger, and Kavin was running out of time.

Kavin's voice echoed through the hospital corridor, "Zara, DON'T DO THAT, ZARA, ZARA!" But his pleas were met with silence. The line was dead, and Zara was gone.

Frustration etched on his face, Kavin turned to his team, "Yuan and Sultan, check Sunil's phone and cabin, everything. Leave no stone unturned."

His eyes locked onto Mr. Kapil's. "Please take care of Sunaina's formalities. She deserves our respect."

With a deep breath, Kavin turned to Rahul and Smith, "You two, come with me. Today, I won't let her win."

The team nodded, their faces set with determination. As they separated to complete their tasks, Rahul and Smith followed Kavin to his car. The tension was palpable, the air thick with anticipation.

Kavin's eyes scanned the surrounding area, his mind racing with possibilities. He knew Zara's gamesand her unpredictability. But he was ready, his resolve strengthened by his team's unwavering support.

As Smith navigated the car through the crowded streets, Kavin's fingers flew across his phone's keypad, dialing a number he knew by heart. The ringtone seemed to stretch on forever before a familiar voice answered.

"Hello, Neel. Where are you? I need your help," Kavin said, his voice tight with tension.

Neel's response was immediate: "I'm home, Kavin. What's wrong?"

Kavin's words tumbled out in a rush, "Track Mithra's number now. Zara has her, and I need to know where they are. Am to your home only"

As Kavin, Smith, and Rahul converged on Neel's home, their faces were etched with determination. But their efforts to track Mithra's number were met with frustration—it was like trying to grasp a wisp of smoke.

Just as they were about to give up, Kavin's phone pierced the air, shrill and insistent. He hesitated for a moment before answering, his voice laced with trepidation. "Hello, Sir."

IG's voice boomed on the other end, "Kavin, what's happening? Sunaina has died."

Kavin's words caught in his throat, guilt and shame choking him. "Sir...that..."

IG's tone turned icy, his frustration palpable. "Did you find the killer or not?"

Kavin took a deep breath, the words tumbling out in a rush. "It's Zara, Sir. We found her, but she escaped and kidnapped Mithra—her last target."

The line went silent, IG's shock almost palpable. "What?"

Kavin's anger flared, his voice low and deadly. "I will find her, Sir."

IG's response was laced with tension. "Kavin, you have to find her and save Mithra."

Kavin's reply was curt, his emotions locked down. "Ok, sir." He didn't reveal the truth—that Mithra was more than just a victim to him.

IG's next words were a bombshell. "The thing is, we found Zoya's dead body in the same graveyard where Advik's father hid it. Lyziden police have arrested him. It confirms that it was Zoya."

Kavin's mind reeled, but his response was stoic. "Ok, sir."

The call ended, leaving Kavin with a sense of foreboding.

Rahul's voice was laced with concern, "Kavin, Sultan called me. He said the media has found out about Sunaina's death and is asking questions. What do we do?"

Kavin's eyes narrowed, his mind racing. After a moment, he responded, "Reveal Zara's photo and Mithra's photo. Tell them everything."

Rahul nodded dutifully, "Ok, I'll inform him."

Kavin's next instructions were crisp: "Block every toll gate and check post. Share the photos with the police and spread them everywhere. She shouldn't escape from Sisalian."

Rahul nodded again, "Ok," and quickly relayed the information to Sultan.

Within hours, the photos of Zara and Mithra were plastered across every news channel and social media platform. The police were on high alert, and every check post was barricaded. The usually lax security was replaced with a sense of urgency, as officers scrutinized every passing vehicle.

The net was tightening around Zara, and Kavin's determination was palpable.

Neel's voice was laced with excitement, "Kavin, Zara's been caught on camera! We're tracking her vehicle now!"

Kavin's phone rang, shrill in the tense moment. He answered, his voice firm. "Hello?"

Kapil's voice was low and urgent, "Kavin, Zara's father has come to the police station."

Kavin's eyes widened in shock. "What? Zara's father?"

Kapil's response was cryptic: "Just come fast, Kavin."

Kavin's mind racing, he ended the call with a curt, "Ok, I'm coming."

He turned to his team, his instructions swift: "Rahul and Smith, go to the location where Zara is hiding. Neel, help them track her down."

With that, Kavin rushed out, his heart pounding in his chest.

Kavin's eyes widened as he entered the police station, Zara's father waiting for him, accompanied by Kapil. But something didn't add up. "Are you Zara's father? But he died in a car accident," Kavin asked, confusion etched on his face.

The man's eyes, though sightless, seemed to hold a deep sorrow. "Yes, that's my brother. I'm Zoya's father. I lost my eyesight in the same accident when Zoya died, and I lost my wife too. Zara took care of me, pretending to be Zoya in front of me, but I knew it was her."

Kavin's mind reeled as the man's story unfolded. "Ok, did you know about her..." Kavin started to ask.

The man's voice cracked, "Yes, two days ago, I had an eye transplant, and today I saw the first thing—her on TV, the murders...and she left a handwritten letter for me."

Kavin's gaze locked onto the man's, his eyes welling up with tears. "Where is the letter?" Kavin asked gently.

The man handed it over, his hands shaking. Kavin took it, his heart heavy with the weight of the man's pain and betrayal.

47

Dear Dad,

I'm overjoyed that you can still see the world through those beautiful eyes of yours, but my heart aches knowing you can't see me, not truly. That's why I'm writing this letter, hoping you'll read my words and understand.

Dad, I'm sorry to confess that I've been living a lie. I'm not Zoya, but Zara. The truth is, Zoya passed away two years ago, and her death was no accident—she was pushed to take her own life.

I'm grateful that you never noticed the difference between us. Your love and acceptance mean everything to me. I feel blessed to have a father like you.

But now, I must make things right. I promise to uncover the truth behind Zoya's tragic end and bring those responsible to justice. I vow to find her remains and give her the proper farewell she deserves. And to those who wronged her, I swear they will face their demise.

With all my love,

- Zara

Kavin's eyes welled up with tears as he read the letter, his heart heavy with sorrow. He looked up to see his father, his eyes brimming with tears, his face etched with pain and regret.

"Please, sir, have mercy! Zara's good soul; she never meant to harm anyone. Don't take her life, I beg of you!" her father implored, tears streaming down his face.

Kavin's expression remained resolute. "She's taken five lives and kidnapped an innocent girl. I'm afraid her actions have consequences."

Her father fell to his knees, desperation etched on his face. "Take my life instead, please! I'll do anything, just spare my daughter. She'll listen to me, I promise. She won't harm anyone else."

Kavin's voice was firm but laced with a hint of empathy. "I'm sorry, sir. It's not possible to trade lives. But I can offer a reprieve. If she surrenders peacefully, I can postpone her punishment. However, my team has already surrounded her location. If she attempts to escape, they have orders to shoot."

Her father grasped at the glimmer of hope. "No, sir, she won't try to escape. I'll talk to her, I promise. She'll listen."

Kavin nodded. "Very well, I'll try to contact her." He dialed Zara's number.

Kavin's face fell as he announced, "She's not reachable." Her father's eyes widened in distress. "What do I do now?"

Just as desperation seemed to consume him, Zara's voice crackled to life on the line. Kavin's grip on the phone tightened, sensing an opportunity. "Where's my father?" Zara demanded, her tone razor-sharp.

"He's with us," Kavin replied, his mind racing with a plan to apprehend her.

Zara's voice dripped with venom. "Did you forget about your girlfriend?"

Kavin swiftly handed the phone to her father, who took it with trembling hands. "Zara, dear..." he began, his voice cracking with emotion.

"Dad, where are you? Did they hurt you?" Zara's concern was palpable.

"No, I'm fine, Zara. Listen to me..." her father pleaded, his words laced with urgency.

As her father's pleas crackled through the phone line, Zara's world began to crumble. "Please surrender yourself," he begged, his voice shattering like fragile glass.

But the words he couldn't bring himself to say hung in the air like a challenge. The weight of his sorrow was too much to bear, and he handed the phone to Kavin, his body wracked with sobs.

Zara's voice was frozen in shock, her words stuck in her throat like a scream that couldn't escape. All she could hear was her father's anguished crying, the sound echoing through her very being like a mournful dirge.

And then, in a moment of devastating defeat, Zara spoke the words that would seal her fate. "Okay, Kavin. Arrest me."

The line went dead, leaving Kavin to wonder at the shattered remains of a father-daughter bond.

❧

As Mithra struggled against the ropes that bound her to the chair, her voice echoed through the room in a desperate plea: "Leave me!" But Zara's anguish and fury would not be silenced.

Tears streaming down her face, Zara's voice cracked with rage: "Because of you, all of this happened!"

Mithra's face contorted in a mixture of pain and guilt as she sobbed, "I know... I know..." The weight of her regret was crushing her, the pang of guilt threatening to consume her.

Zara's words cut deep, a relentless barrage of sorrow and anger: "If only you had been her friend, supported her, treated her with kindness, and helped her that day... she would be alive and happy now. All because of you!" The phrase became a refrain, a haunting reminder of what could have been.

As Zara's words trailed off, she collapsed to the floor, overwhelmed by grief. Mithra's voice was barely audible, a trembling whisper: "I'm sorry..."

But Zara's forgiveness was not forthcoming. Instead, her anger flared anew: "I won't forgive you! You took away her first love, her peace, her life, and tarnished her name!" The words were a lash, striking Mithra with the force of Zara's fury.

Mithra winced, feeling the sting of Zara's condemnation. "Please, don't kill me with your words," she begged, her voice cracking.

But Zara was unyielding: "What I'm saying is what you did."

As the sun began to set on the small town, casting a golden glow over the streets, Kavin and the police force closed in onto the location where Zara was hiding. The air was thick with tension; the only sound was the soft crunch of gravel beneath their feet.

৪৩

Kavin, his eyes fixed intently on the building ahead, led the way. His heart raced with anticipation, his mind racing with thoughts of finally bringing Zara to justice.

The police officers flanked him, their faces set with determination. They had been searching for Zara for weeks, following every lead, every tip. And finally, they found her.

As they approached the entrance, Kavin signaled for the officers to fan out, surrounding the building. He took a deep breath, his hand on the door handle.

"Let's do this," he whispered, pushing open the door.

The officers poured in behind him, their flashlights casting flickering shadows on the walls. Kavin's eyes scanned the room, locking onto a figure huddled in the corner.

"Zara," he said, his voice firm. "It's over."

But as he approached her, he saw something that made his heart skip a beat. A look of defiance in her eyes, a small smile playing on her lips.

"You turned my father against me, Kavin," she said, her voice dripping with malice.

"Zara, listen to me," Kavin said, his voice firm but laced with empathy. "You took the law into your own hands, and that's not right. You can't avenge Zoya's death by hurting others."

Zara's eyes welled up with tears as she asked, her voice trembling, "Did you finally find out what happened to Zoya?"

Kavin's expression turned somber. "We found her dead body, and we arrested Advik's father in connection with her murder."

Zara's face contorted in a mixture of sorrow and shock, her smile a heartbreaking contradiction. "What? Arrest?" she whispered as if the word itself was a cruel joke.

"He inflicts a cruel punishment that instills fear in everyone!" Zara exclaimed, her rage boiling over.

"Okay, I promise to release Mithra," Kavin said, seeing Mithra tied to a chair.

"Who will punish Mithra, then?" Zara demanded, her anger intensified. "She's the root of all this! I won't believe you!" Zara's fury reached a breaking point as she pointed a gun at Kavin.

"Zara, put your gun down; don't do this!" Kavin pleaded.

"No, you'll just save her, I know!" Zara spat, loading her gun. She kept the weapon trained on the police team. "Zara, don't do this; put your gun down!" her father urged.

"Dad, don't believe them!" Zara cried, her finger tightening on the trigger. She fired a shot, and the sound of continuous gunfire filled the air. The loud reports sent birds fleeing in terror, their startled squawks echoing through the surrounding area.

48

As the chaos unfolded, Zara's gunshots rang out, striking Rahul with precision. He crumpled to the ground, his body limp and lifeless. Smith rushed to his side, holding him tight as blood seeped from the wound on his chest. Rahul's eyes fluttered closely, his body going still as he lost consciousness.

Meanwhile, the police returned fire, their bullets finding their mark on Zara's body. She stumbled backwards, her gun falling from her grasp as she attempted to clutch at her wounds. The rapid gunfire was relentless, and Zara's body jerked violently before collapsing to the ground. She lay there, her eyes frozen in a permanent stare, her life extinguished in an instant.

Her father's anguished scream pierced the air as he rushed to his daughter's side. He cradled her lifeless body in his lap, tears streaming down his face as he rocked back and forth in grief. "Zara, my child, my child!" he wailed, his voice cracking with despair.

As the police approached, they quickly untied Mithra, freeing her from her restraints. She stumbled forward, her eyes wide with shock and horror at the scene before her. The air was heavy with the smell of smoke and blood, and the sound of sirens echoed in the distance, a stark reminder of the destruction that had unfolded.

Amid the chaos, Smith held Rahul's limp form, his face etched with worry and fear. "Rahul, please, don't leave me," he whispered, his voice trembling with emotion. The outcome was far from certain, leaving only uncertainty and heartache in its wake.

"Take him to the hospital, fast!" Kavin urged, his voice laced with concern.

The paramedics sprang into action, swiftly loading Rahul into the ambulance. Mithra, still shaken, was helped into the vehicle alongside him. Meanwhile, Zara's lifeless body was carefully placed in a separate compartment, her father's anguished cries echoing through the air as he accompanied her.

The ambulance sped away, sirens blaring, as the scene of chaos and destruction was left behind. The hospital's emergency team was already on standby, ready to receive the wounded and the dead.

As the ambulance doors burst open, the hospital's emergency team sprang into action. Rahul, still unconscious and critically injured, was swiftly whisked away to the emergency ward. The doctors and nurses moved with precision, their faces set with concern.

Meanwhile, Zara's lifeless body was taken to the autopsy room, her father's anguished cries still echoing in the air. He sat down, his head in his hands, his body weakened by the shock and grief. His blood pressure had plummeted, leaving him feeling faint and disoriented.

Rahul was rushed into surgery, and the medical team was fighting to save his life. Mithra, traumatized by the events, was taken to a quiet room, surrounded by counselors and medical staff. They worked to calm her shattered nerves, helping her process the horror she had witnessed.

The hospital's corridors were abuzz with activity, filled with the sound of urgent whispers, the beeping of machines, and the soft murmur of sorrow. The media had descended upon the hospital, reporters and camera crews clamoring for information. Police officers stood guard, their faces stern and alert, as they worked to piece together the events of the tragic day.

The atmosphere was tense, the air thick with worry and uncertainty. Kavin, Smith, and the medical staff waited anxiously for news from the surgery room, their hearts heavy with concern for Rahul's fate.

As the news spread like wildfire, the hospital was inundated with a flurry of anxious visitors. Yuan and Sultan rushed in, their faces etched with worry, asking about Rahul's condition. "How is he? Is he going to make it?" they asked in unison, their voices laced with concern.

Meanwhile, Manasvi, Neel, Nithin, Aarav, and Vibha arrived, their faces tense with emotion. Despite Zara's dark secrets as a serial killer, she was still their friend, and the news of her demise had left them reeling. They gathered around Mithra, offering comfort and support as she struggled to come to terms with the traumatic events.

The hospital's corridors were filled with a cacophony of emotions—shock, grief, worry, and concern. Friends and acquaintances mingled, sharing tears and stories, trying to make sense of the senseless tragedy. The air was heavy with sorrow as the community came together to support one another in their time of need.

As the crowd swelled, the hospital's staff worked tirelessly to maintain order, ensuring that the patients received the care they needed. The sound of whispers, sobs, and murmured conversations filled the air, creating a sense of collective heartache. Amidst the chaos, one thing was clear: the bonds of friendship and community would help them navigate even the darkest of times.

Mithra lay on the hospital bed, and her wound was being tended to by the medical staff. Her friends surrounded her, their faces etched with concern and worry. Manasvi, tears streaming down her face, asked, "Mithra, are you okay?"

Mithra's voice trembled as she replied, "I'm fine... don't worry about me." She paused, her emotions overwhelming her. "It's just... Zoya, Zara, and so many others... they're gone." Her body shook with sobs as she hugged Manasvi tightly.

The group of friends closed in, trying to offer comfort and solace. They stroked her hair, held her hands, and whispered words of encouragement, attempting to ease her pain. Neel, Nithin, Aarav, and Vibha all tried to console her, their faces reflecting their grief and shock.

Meanwhile, Kavin stood apart, his eyes scanning the hospital room as if searching for something or someone. His expression was a mix of concern and distraction, his mind seemingly elsewhere.

The scene was one of collective heartache, as the friends struggled to come to terms with the trauma they had endured. Mithra's tears were contagious, and soon the entire group was overcome with emotion, mourning the loss of their friends and the shattered innocence of their lives.

"Where is Kavin?" Aarav asked, scanning the room with a hint of concern.

Mithra's response was barely audible, her voice choked with emotion. "He's... he's probably checking on Rahul. He was seriously injured... shot by Zara... and he's in the emergency room." Her words trailed off as she succumbed to a fresh wave of tears.

The pain, guilt, and sense of loss threatened to consume her, each emotion warring for dominance. The physical wound she had suffered seemed trivial compared to the anguish that ravaged her heart and mind. The weight of her grief was crushing her, making it hard to breathe and hard to think.

As she sobbed, her friends closed in, offering what little comfort they could. They held her, stroked her hair, and whispered words of solace, but Mithra felt lost, adrift in a sea of despair. The thought of Rahul's condition, of Zara's betrayal, and of the lives forever changed by that fateful day were almost too much to bear.

After an agonizing wait, the surgical team finally emerged with news of Rahul's condition. "He's going to make it," the doctor announced, a hint of a smile on his face. "He's still unconscious, but we've managed to stabilize him. He was close to death's door, but he's been pulled back."

Smith and the team breathed a collective sigh of relief as the doctor continued, "He'll take some time to recover, but don't worry; he'll be fine. We just need to monitor him closely and ensure he gets the rest he needs."

As the medical team began to disperse, Smith and the others lingered, their faces etched with a mix of exhaustion and gratitude. They had come close to losing Rahul, but fate had given them a second chance.

With renewed determination, they set out to complete their incomplete duties, fueled by a sense of purpose and a deeper appreciation for life. The ordeal had left its mark, but they were determined to emerge stronger and more united than ever.

Kavin stood outside Mithra's hospital room, gazing at her through the glass window. She attempted a weak smile, but the pain and sorrow in her eyes were unmistakable. Kavin's heart ached as he beheld her fragile state, the weight of her suffering palpable even from a distance.

Without mustering the courage to enter the room, Kavin turned away, his footsteps echoing down the deserted corridor. He couldn't bring himself to face her, not yet. The guilt and regret that had been building up inside him seemed too much to bear.

As he walked away, Kavin couldn't shake off the image of Mithra's pain-filled eyes, a haunting reminder of the turmoil that had ravaged their lives.

49

The day of reckoning had finally arrived, and the courtroom was abuzz with anticipation. The media and crowds of people thronged the premises, eager to witness the judgment. Kavin and his team, minus Rahul, who was still recovering in the hospital, stood nervously, awaiting the verdict.

The courtroom was packed with familiar faces—Zoya's father and Aunty Jo, Advik's father, Kiara's parents, and even the cake shop owner, all of whom had been impacted by the tragic events. Each person present had a stake in the outcome; their lives were forever changed by the actions of Zara and her accomplices.

As the judge entered the courtroom, the crowd rose to their feet in a show of respect. But before the judge could take their seat, a surprise twist emerged. Prosecutor Nithin strode confidently into the room, with a determined look on his face.

With a deep breath, Nithin began to present his case, revealing shocking new evidence. He alleged that Advik's father had knowingly concealed his son's heinous crimes, including the rape and murder of Zoya. Nithin argued that Advik's father had callously prioritized his family's reputation over justice, allowing his son to escape accountability for his monstrous acts.

Nithin's voice rang out across the courtroom, his words hanging in the air like a challenge. "I request that the court hold Advik's father accountable for his role in covering up these atrocities. He must be punished for his complicity in Zoya's tragic demise and the subsequent cover-up."

The courtroom erupted into chaos, with gasps and murmurs spreading like wildfire. Advik's father's face turned ashen, his eyes darting wildly as he realized the gravity of the accusations against him.

Nithin's zealous presentation continued, shedding light on another dark chapter. He exposed the drug supplier who had been peddling narcotics to school students, including Harsha, who had succumbed to the allure of substance abuse. The courtroom listened with rapt attention as Nithin revealed the supplier's nefarious activities, which had led to the downfall of many young lives.

With unyielding conviction, Nithin demanded justice for the victims and their families. "I request that the court meet out the severest punishment to this drug supplier, who has ravaged the lives of innocent students. His actions have left irreparable scars, and he must be held accountable for the destruction he has caused."

"Doctor Sunil has committed a heinous medical crime," Nithin declared, his voice firm and resolute in the courtroom. Zara blackmailed him, exploiting his vulnerabilities to manipulate him into killing Sunaina. He succumbed to her pressure, carrying out the deed in the hospital room, following the same twisted pattern that Zara has consistently employed."

Nithin's words hung in the air, painting a damning picture of Doctor Sunil's complicity in the crime. The judge's expression turned grave, weighing the severity of the accusation.

"And then, consumed by the weight of his guilt and shame, Doctor Sunil took his own life in his cabin," Nithin concluded, his voice heavy with the gravity of the revelation.

The judge's voice cut through the silence, commanding attention from all present. The courtroom fell still, the air thick with anticipation, as the judge began to deliver the verdict.

"The court hereby orders that a compensation fund be established for the victims' families, to provide them with some measure of support and comfort in their time of grief," the judge declared.

Regarding Advik's father, the judge's words were stern: "For his role in concealing evidence and hindering the investigation, Advik's father is hereby sentenced to life imprisonment. His actions have shown a blatant disregard for the law and the well-being of others, and he must face the consequences."

The judge then turned their attention to the drug supplier, their voice unwavering as they read out the relevant law section: "According to Section 27 of the Narcotic Drugs and Psychotropic Substances Act, any person found guilty of supplying drugs to minors shall be punishable with rigorous imprisonment for a term that shall not be less than ten years but may extend to twenty years and shall also be liable to a fine."

"The police shall conduct a thorough investigation into the hospital's corruption, and this case shall be tried separately in court," the judge declared, his voice firm and authoritative as he banged his gavel.

The courtroom fell silent once more, the weight of the judge's words sinking in.

"The court will arrange for a doctor and psychiatrist to provide treatment and support to the drug-addicted student to help them overcome their addiction and rebuild their life."

The judge also acknowledged the bravery of Police Officer Rahul, who had suffered injuries while apprehending the killer: "A fund has been established to support Officer Rahul's recovery and recognize his valor in the line of duty."

The judge then turned to the secret group, who had played a crucial role in uncovering the truth: "The secret group has done an outstanding job in uncovering the hidden puzzles and bringing the perpetrators to justice. They are hereby honored with medals for their exceptional service."

The judge also offered some parting words of wisdom: "This case serves as a stark reminder that schools must be vigilant and proactive in monitoring their students' activities, and parents must pay attention to their children's behavior and well-being."

With that, the judge banged their gavel, signalling the conclusion of the case: "The court is dismissed."

The news of the Sisalin killer's background sent shockwaves across the nation, breaking the hearts of everyone who heard it. The channels were flooded with breaking news updates, revealing the tragic and disturbing details of the killer's past.

As the news spread like wildfire, people from all walks of life were left stunned and saddened by the revelations. The killer's backstory, marked by trauma, neglect, and pain, was a poignant reminder of the devastating consequences of unchecked suffering and the importance of addressing the root causes of violence.

They emerged from the courtroom with a mix of pride and sadness, their faces etched with a sense of somber triumph. Pride in the fact that justice had been served, and sadness for the loss of Zara, whose life had been brutally cut short.

It was a moment of triumph and closure for Kavin as he entered the hospital ward where Mithra lay recovering. His eyes welled up with tears, and a proud smile spread across his face. He approached Mithra's bedside, surrounded by their friends, and asked, "Mithra, how's your health?"

Mithra's weak but determined voice replied, "Fine." Kavin's gaze locked onto hers, filled with compassion and understanding. "Mithra, don't feel guilty anymore. Everything is over. Zoya will be happy and rest in peace," he said, trying to console her.

Mithra's eyes brimmed with tears as she asked, "Will Zoya forgive me?" Kavin's expression turned gentle, and he said, "Why not, Mithra? You solved the unsolved cube." A faint smile appeared on her lips.

With a tender gesture, Kavin knelt beside her bed and pulled out a small ring box from his pocket. "Mithra, will you marry me?" He proposed, his voice filled with emotion.

Mithra's smile grew wider, and she teased, "What if I say no?" Kavin's face lit up with mock seriousness, "I'll kidnap you!" The room erupted in laughter, and Mithra's eyes sparkled with happiness as she nodded to her consent.

As Kavin slipped the ring onto Mithra's finger, the room was filled with a collective "aww" from their friends. Mithra's eyes shone with tears of joy, and a radiant smile spread across her face.

Kavin's eyes locked onto hers, filled with love and adoration, as he wrapped his arms around her in a tight embrace. The two shared a tender, heartfelt hug, basking in the warmth of their love.

The hospital ward, once a place of recovery and healing, had transformed into a sanctuary of hope and new beginnings. The friends surrounding them cheered and applauded, celebrating the union of the two souls.

Vibha gazed at Aarav with a knowing smile, her eyes sparkling with amusement. Aarav, oblivious to the tender moment that had just unfolded, turned to her with a curious expression. "What happened?" he asked, seeking clarification.

Vibha's smile grew wider as she leaned in, her voice barely above a whisper. "Nothing... He never understood," she murmured, her words dripping with playful sarcasm.

The air was electric as Aarav's warm breath caressed Vibha's ear, his whispered question sending shivers down her spine. "Do you like to kiss?" he asked, his voice husky and intimate.

Vibha's eyes widened in surprise, her heart racing as she turned to face him. Aarav's proximity was unnerving, their faces inches apart, the space between them charged with tension.

Without waiting for a response, Aarav's lips brushed against Vibha's, sending sparks flying. The gentle touch ignited a flutter in her chest, and to his delight, he felt her smile beneath his lips.

The world around them melted away, leaving only the two of them, lost in the magic of their first kiss. Time stood still, and all that existed was the soft, tender touch of their lips.

"I love you," Aarav proposed to her. She hugged him tightly. "I love you so much.".

Neel's teasing voice cut through the air, "Aahh haa, I knew you two would end up in love!" Vibha's face turned bright red as Sarah playfully held her hands, grinning from ear to ear.

Neel continued, "Kavin, you know there are now three couples among us!" Kavin's curiosity was piqued. "What? Who?" he asked, his eyes scanning the group.

Neel announced, "Nithin finally expressed his love to Manasvi!" Kavin's face lit up with a warm smile, "Wow, that's amazing!" He was genuinely happy for the new couple.

The group erupted in a chorus of congratulations and cheers, basking in the joy of new love and friendship. The atmosphere was electric, filled with laughter and excitement, as they celebrated the blossoming relationships among them.

℘

Days later, the small town of Lyziden was filled with mourners who had gathered to pay their respects to Zoya and Zara. Kavin and his team, who had worked tirelessly to bring the perpetrators to justice, were in attendance, their faces somber and reflective.

Rahul, who had made a remarkable recovery from his injuries, was also present, his eyes cast downward in reverence. Mithra, Zoya's closest friend, was there, surrounded by their mutual friends, all of whom had been deeply affected by the tragedy.

The atmosphere was heavy with grief as the community came together to bid a final farewell to the two young lives that had been senselessly lost. The funeral procession was a poignant reminder of the devastating impact of the tragedy, and the outpouring of support was a testament to the love and respect that Zoya and Zara had earned in their short lives. The funeral was decorated with Gerbera daisies.

℘

As the mourners gathered around the gravesite, they shared stories, memories, and tears, celebrating the lives of the two young women who had left an indelible mark on their hearts.

The funeral procession was a somber affair, with everyone present paying their respects to Zoya and Zara. The atmosphere was heavy with grief, and the weight of their loss hung in the air like a palpable mist.

Zoya's father, overcome with sorrow, sat amidst the orphanage children, his eyes red from crying. Mithra approached him, her own eyes brimming with tears, and begging for forgiveness. "Uncle, please forgive me," she implored, her voice barely above a whisper.

But Zoya's father, with a deep understanding and compassion, placed a gentle hand on Mithra's shoulder. "Mithra, that was not a mistake that happened at that age. What happened to Zoya was a tragedy, a senseless act that cannot be blamed on anyone but the perpetrator. Stop blaming yourself for everything," he said, his words filled with empathy.

As he rose to attend to the guests, his words struck a chord within Mithra. The weight of her guilt, which had been crushing her, began to lift. She felt a sense of liberation, a realization that she was not responsible for the tragedy that had unfolded.

The words of Zoya's father were like a balm to Mithra's soul, soothing her grief and guilt. She felt a sense of peace wash over her, and her eyes, though still tearful, shone with a newfound hope.

Mithra sat beside Zoya's grave, her eyes fixed on the inscription that bore her friend's name. She took a deep breath, and with a quivering voice, began to speak. Zoya, I'm sorry if I could be your friend. I know you wanted me to be smiling, to express my inner feelings."

She paused, collecting her thoughts, and continued, "I learned, and I solved." From her handbag, she retrieved the cube that had been a symbol of their friendship and Zoya's unsolved dreams. With trembling hands, she placed it on the grave.

"I solved the unsolved cube," she whispered, her voice cracking with emotion. Tears began to fall from her eyes, streaming down her face as she finally let go of the guilt and grief that had been holding her back.

With a sense of closure, Mithra stood up, her eyes never leaving the grave. She took one last look at the cube, now a symbol of her growth and healing, and turned to walk away, the weight of her sorrow slowly lifting with each step.

As Mithra turned to walk away, she glanced back at Zoya's grave, and a gentle smile spread across her face. The tears still glistened on her cheeks, but her eyes shone with a sense of peace and closure.